Call Me
Lion

Camilla.

Call Me
Lion

Camilla Chester

Firefly

First published in 2022
by Firefly Press
25 Gabalfa Road, Llandaff North, Cardiff, CF14 2JJ
www.fireflypress.co.uk

A CIP catalogue record of this book is available from
the British Library.

1 3 5 7 9 8 6 4 2

ISBN 978-1-913102-89-0

This book has been published with the support of
the Books Council of Wales.

Typeset by: Elaine Sharples

Printed by CPI Group (UK) Ltd, Croydon, Surrey, CR0 4YY

In memory of James John Redrup,
a lover of lions.
1989 - 2014

1

Even though my trampoline is in the shade, the heatwave makes it too hot for bouncing. I bounce anyway because when you have no friends in the summer holidays there's nothing else to do.

'Hello!'

It's a girl's voice. It comes with a body and a grinning face that bobs up and down behind the third fence panel along. The new neighbours must have a trampoline exactly in line with ours. It feels like an invasion.

'I'm Richa,' says the girl and waves when she's at her highest. Her hair is black and long. It stays in the air after she falls, like an exclamation mark above her head.

The urge to run and hide is strong, but I force myself to keep bouncing.

My dog, Patch, gets up and sticks his nose under the fence. His tail wags really fast and he makes a 'hello' whine.

Richa notices him when she's up above the fence. She points and says, 'You've got a dog! I love dogs, but my stupid brother Aahan is allergic. He's a totally useless three year old who cries and moans and carries on and on about nothing.' Richa's voice is hot and puffy. It goes quiet and loud depending on where she is in the air. She sounds like she's from somewhere different. Not Luton. 'I'm ten,' she goes on. 'How old are you? What's your dog called?'

She's good at bouncing. She's good at talking. She has long, thin arms that waggle about streaked with sun cream, and bare feet. Like everyone she wears shorts and a vest top. Because of the heatwave all clothes make you boiling hot. The only shoes people wear are flip-flops or sandals.

One of the back windows of Richa's house opens wider. A woman, who is probably Richa's mum, leans out and speaks a whole load of words in another language.

There are lots of kids from all over the world at my school. My guess is that Richa's mum is speaking in Gujarati, because she speaks just like Rama in Chestnut Class and his family are from Gujarat in India.

If I could talk, it might be a question I would ask Richa, but I will never ask a question to a stranger. It's hard enough just to keep bouncing and not run away, and I can only look at Richa when she isn't looking at me.

Richa shouts back in one big rush. She says three words in English: 'roasting', 'bouncing' and 'dog'. Their conversation carries on, sounding crosser all the time until Richa stops it by saying, 'na, na' and bouncing around so that her back is turned to the window.

'She wants to slam the window shut to show she's angry with me,' Richa explains, 'but it's way too boiling hot for closed windows. She'll shut the curtains all huffy instead.'

Boiling and roasting are words that everyone

uses. We know the heatwave is cooking us all, like sausages.

'Mum says it's hotter than India,' Richa says, still bouncing. 'She's grumpy because we've had to move house and she's really, really, *really* pregnant. I hope it's a girl.' She looks me up and down between bounces and adds, 'No offence. Not all boys are bad, but I do-not-want-another-brother!' Richa says the last bit up into the sky with her hands in prayer.

She bounces a bit more, watching me, then says, 'Do you have any brothers or sisters? You don't say much. Don't you talk? Why don't you talk?'

It's amazing to me that Richa can say all these words. If I was a boy that could speak, these would be my answers to her questions:

1. My name is Leo, but the people I can talk to call me Lion. I can count all of their names on one hand.
2. I'm ten too. Just had my birthday party with my family. It was OK, and nothing like Theo's party at *RollerCentral* where I froze like a statue and everybody stared at me. That was the worst time of my entire life.

4

3. My dog is called Patch because he is brown and white but has a big black patch over his right eye and ear. It makes him look like a dog-pirate. I can talk to Patch. He is my only one true friend. What I would like more than anything in the whole world is a real friend, but you can't be friends with someone who can't talk – fact.

4. I have a big brother called Ryan who is seventeen and sprays stuff all over his body that makes the back of my throat go dry. Brianne is my sister; she is sixteen and wears floaty skirts and scarves and wants to be a physicist. Brianne and Ryan argue all the time.

5. No, I don't say much. I want to talk but I can't.

2

Richa doesn't seem bothered that I can't answer any of her questions. She keeps chatting and bouncing and asking me things.

The worry that Richa is there eases and I stop wanting to run away and hide. It starts to get fun, despite the heat. I like the whoosh of air lifting my hair, the roar in my ears and the light feeling in my body.

Bouncing is good, but not as free as dancing. I go to dance class once a week and Just Jive, my summer dance school, starts on Monday. Three brilliant weeks of dancing. Last year there was a Just Jive show. I really wanted to perform but my Selective Mutism stopped me. The thought of the class and my fun teacher, Felicity Delaware, makes me do dance-jumps.

I jump in a big star and a pogo stick. I do a scissor kick, and a lightning bolt.

As I dance-jump Richa stops talking. I'd got almost used to her chattering away. I twist jump to face her. She twists too, matching my move. We jump, facing each other, perfectly in sync. I try a star and she copies me, stretching her arms and legs out wide. Next, I jump a superman; Richa mimics me, her right arm straight up, fist tightly clenched. She matches a couple of straight jumps, then a quick-tuck. Both our knees are hugged tight into our chests. There's a good feeling inside me.

She laughs. 'I'm as quick as you. My turn!'

I copy a few of Richa's straight 'jump into the swimming pool' style bounces, arms clamped tight to our sides. Then I copy her back-leg flick and a knee-bounce.

It's fun.

She pokes out her tongue, I copy. I wave my arms in the air above my head, she copies. She makes floppy bunny ears, I copy. She goes crazy, freestyle, wobbly mad and does lots and lots of bounces. She keeps laughing and laughing and saying, 'That's not the same. You got it wrong.'

I grin and almost laugh. This is the most fun I've had with anyone who can't call me Lion in a long time, maybe ever.

After a lot of different bounces and dance moves, Richa flops onto her belly on her trampoline. I have to bounce up high to see her.

'I'm too hot,' she complains. 'There's only boring water in our house. And it's all warm from the tap. No ice. We've not got the freezer bit of the fridge working properly yet.' She rolls onto her back, squints her eyes against the glaring sun above and announces, 'I'm coming over to your house.'

Panic stops my bouncing. Out of rhythm, the trampoline bullies me, bumping me to my knees and flat onto my belly. I hear Richa call up to the open window, probably telling her mum in Gujarati where she's going. Her mum leans out again and looks over our fence.

She says, 'Alright with you?' to me, her Indian accent heavy. I see the top of her belly all stretched with baby.

'He doesn't talk, Ma,' Richa shouts up.

'What?'

Richa answers her in Gujarati. Her mum answers back.

'Alright, half an hour. I get it. OK,' Richa says, and I hear her crunching her way through the wildly dried-up, crispy plants in her garden to her back gate. I swivel round to sit on the edge of my trampoline, my legs swinging free, my heart racing. Patch rushes down our garden to greet Richa as she comes through our gate and closes it behind her. The confidence of this amazes me. She acts if she has always lived here and does this every day.

'Look at you!' Richa says as Patch leaps all over her, trying to lick her bare legs and wagging his tail so fast all his body goes bendy. 'What a good boy. You are a lovely dog. Look at your patch.'

Dogs know lots of words, at least fifty scientists say, and definitely their own names. When Patch hears his name, he squeals with happiness as if he's been waiting for Richa to arrive his whole life.

'Is that your name? Are you called Patch? What a beautiful boy. What a good boy you are Patchy Patch Patch.'

Patch rolls onto his back showing his white belly, his tongue lolling out the side of his mouth his feet bent over, desperate for more and more tummy tickles.

'Hello, hello.' Ryan appears, framed by the back doorway, eating what I call Napoleon (even though I know it is supposed to be called Neapolitan) ice cream, straight from the tub.

Grateful to be distracted from Richa for a minute, I jump down to take a look, making sure my brother isn't scoffing only the chocolate. He is. It smells good and I want him to share, but can't ask him, not with Richa here.

'Who's your friend, Lion?' Ryan asks me, nodding down the garden towards Richa.

'Lion?' says Richa, getting up from petting Patch. 'Is that your real name?' she asks me. She tries to walk towards us but it's difficult for her to get close with Patch weaving in front of her and staring up at her like she's the Goddess of all dogs. I thought he only looked at me like that. All kinds of confusing thoughts and feelings are rushing through me. It's impossible to pick just one, but my worry gets stronger the nearer Richa gets.

Ryan leaves the spoon in his mouth so he can pat my head. I know this means that my brother will tell Richa about my hair and there's nothing I can do to stop him. I watch Ryan dig the licked spoon back into what's left of the chocolate ice cream.

'When Leo was born,' Ryan begins, drawing Richa closer, 'he had a full head of hair. It puffed up high and when our sister, Brianne, first saw it she said it looked like a dandelion clock – you know, like the ones you blow on to tell the time?'

'I know them, but they're rubbish,' says Richa, 'they never work. I just use a watch.'

Ryan chuckles. 'Anyway, he got called Lion, short for Dandelion, because of his hair. He's been Lion ever since.'

'But your real name is Leo?' Richa asks me. I stare at her knees, all dusty from where she's been kneeling to play with Patch. She's getting closer so my worry should still be getting bigger, but it's not. My worry is staying still. She's near enough for me to catch the coconut scent of her sun cream.

'He won't talk to you,' Ryan explains.

I can feel Richa studying my hair. 'It looks like a lion's mane,' she decides.

I like the idea of a lion's mane better than a dandelion clock and I wish I could tell her that. Someday, somehow, I'm going to overcome my Selective Mutism enough to perform. I want to dance in *The Lion King* in the West End. It feels like a step towards my dream if I've already got the right hair.

'I'm Ryan, older brother.' He sticks the spoon back in his mouth and offers his hand like he's making a business deal.

'Richa,' says Richa, shaking it. 'Moved in next door.'

'From somewhere in the north, is it?'

Richa nods. 'We've lived all over the place, but this is our first time in the south.'

'Well, welcome to St Dukes Estate. Luton's finest.' He sounds funny because he still has the spoon in his mouth. He takes it out and wiggles it at Richa. 'No brothers or sisters?'

'I've a ratty little brother and Mum's about to have a baby.'

'Nice,' says Ryan. 'Thirsty?'

Richa nods. 'Dry as Weetabix ... without milk.'

Ryan laughs. 'Funny girl. I like you. Got a good one here, Lion.'

I've spent hours imagining having a friend. I even practise imaginary friend conversations with Patch. My sister Brianne says that when you read, you're never alone: not really, because you make friends with all the characters in the stories. She taught me to read and write before I started school. I'm brilliant at it. Reading and writing is how I talk when I'm not with family.

But it's easy for Brianne to say that to me, because she has lots of real friends that she can talk to.

What the kids at school say is definitely true: you can't be friends with someone who can't talk. It's impossible, but it doesn't stop me from dreaming about it.

3

'What's your poison?' Ryan asks Richa opening the fridge and doing his head-popping dance move.

Ryan is a good dancer: he calls it 'busting moves'.

'Got any pop?' Richa asks.

Ryan takes out a big bottle of lemonade and pours two glasses.

'Maybe add some ice? It's thirty-odd degrees in here,' Brianne says, striding into the kitchen.

Her hair is still damp from the shower and she smells of her fancy shea butter shampoo. Ryan ignores her and hands out the drinks.

'Ugh. You've been eating straight out of the tub again.' Brianne snatches the ice cream off the side, tosses the spoon into the dishwasher and puts the lid back on.

'Hey, I was eating that,' Ryan says.

Brianne answers by handing him the ice-cube tray and putting the ice cream back in the freezer. She turns to Richa all smiles. 'Hi, I'm Brianne, Leo's sister. I'm not actually the eldest but I'm the most mature.' She glares at Ryan.

'Most boring more like,' Ryan retorts.

Brianne ignores him, smiling again at Richa instead. 'You're Richa, right? I've just been talking to your mum out the front. She looks like she's struggling in this heat.' Brianne sighs and shakes her head slowly, making her long earrings sway from side to side.

Richa is guzzling her lemonade, having not bothered waiting for the ice, and doesn't answer my sister. The kitchen feels very busy and full of words. Brianne carries on regardless.

'It will be really nice for Leo to have someone

his own age living next door. You going to Lakeside Primary in September?'

Richa splutters into her lemonade and launches into a coughing fit. Once recovered, she notices my sister's expectant eyes still on her and manages a quick nod.

'That's great!' says Brianne. She claps her hands and her bangles jingle together. 'Leo says Year Sixes are allowed to walk into school without an adult. You two can go together now.'

'We've got the whole holiday first,' Richa protests, almost in a panic. Maybe Richa doesn't like school much either, or maybe she's just worried about the thought of walking in with me.

'Yeah, Brianne,' says Ryan. 'Only nerds, like you, study in the summer. These kids just want to hang out.'

'At least they really are kids,' Brianne bats back.

Ryan grunts and gets the ice cream back out of the freezer.

'What you going to play then?' asks Brianne.

Richa shrugs and glances at me. I know what she's thinking: what games can you play with a boy that doesn't talk?

'You could play Domino Falls. You love that game don't you, Lion?' Brianne says.

Feeling my face heat up, I look at Patch who is sat on Richa's feet having his black ear tickled.

'You could read? Leo has got loads of books.'

Snatching a glance at Richa I can tell from her freaked-out expression that she's thinking of making a break for the door.

'Or you could make mud pies?' suggests Brianne, adding to my embarrassment. 'Once you start digging at the ground Patch will probably join in. He loves digging up the mud for Leo's pies.'

'Way to sell the boy, Brianne,' Ryan says through his ice cream.

Richa laughs and looks more at ease again, but my face is on full burn. This is a total disaster. I try and hide my shame in my lemonade.

'Why don't you suggest something then?' Brianne snaps.

There's a moment of nothing that seems to stretch long, just like the hot of the heatwave.

After Ryan sets up the PlayStation we play Sonic with the windows open but the curtains closed. Patch sits as close to Richa as possible. There's a hot, closed-in smell to the room, sweetened by Richa's coconut sun cream. It's difficult to concentrate on the game, with everything racing around inside me, but I'm still better than Richa. Her player keeps running into walls and off the edges.

'Is it unlimited lives or something?' she asks.

I can't say, so instead I watch her play and puzzle out how to pick up the game again once she's died.

'Imagine if, in real life, you could just start over,' Richa says, scrunching up her face in concentration. 'Every time you made a mistake you could just go back to the beginning and try again. Would you do that, or would you just keep going?'

I'd keep going. I never want to re-live bad things that have happened, like Theo's party, but I can't tell her that.

Richa tells me the reason she is rubbish with games is because her mum and dad won't buy her a phone and that's how everyone learns to play video games. I'd like my own phone too.

It would make a lot of things easier. Richa chats on over the sound effects of the game. She asks and answers her own questions. Looking sideways at her, I start to remember Tiffany. There's a dull ache in my stomach when I think of what happened.

Tiffany was new in our class and didn't know anything about me or my SM. She's really good at football and immediately took over the playground. One day, Tiffany kicked the ball and it came skidding and skipping right over to where I was stood, partly hidden by the trees, watching. The ball hit my shins. It was surprising to me that I felt it. It was like something coming alive out of the TV and I remember just staring at it rolling around me. Tiffany ran towards me and shouted, 'Come on, kick it over. Come on, we're in a game. Just kick it.'

And I did! I kicked it and she cheered and said, 'Come and play, we need someone to mark Theo.'

But I shook my head, because I couldn't climb inside the TV, besides it was Theo and the humiliation of his party was still raw.

I kept watching, though, and pushing myself

to go and join in with the game. Tiffany gave me a few more chances, waving an arm through the air to call me in. I wanted to, but I couldn't.

It got me thinking – maybe Tiffany was different, because I wasn't invisible to her like I was to the other kids. Maybe she could teach me how to play football? I wanted to be part of something and not feel so lonely, so I started to follow Tiffany around. Even when she became friends with Scarlett and Maryam, I still followed her.

There would be a moment at the start of playtime, I thought, when she would say, 'Hello Leo,' all friendly, and grin at me. She'd gently pass me the ball and I would pass it back and she would say, 'Not bad for a beginner'.

But then I heard them talking and everything changed.

'What's up with the pale boy with the big orange hair?' Tiffany asked Scarlett in book corner one afternoon. The shock of hearing me being talked about made me duck behind the shelves. My heart was thumping so loud it almost drowned out their voices. I strained to listen, wanting to hear but dreading it at the same time.

'You mean Leo?' Scarlett said.

'Yeah. I think he's following me about. It's a bit odd,' said Tiffany.

'He has a thing,' Scarlett explained.

'What do you mean? Is he autistic or something? He doesn't say anything, ever.'

'That's his thing. He doesn't talk. Mrs Malik told us all about it in Year Two. He's got mutism something. He's terrified of talking. It makes him a loner because it stops him from making friends.'

'Why's he following me?' Tiffany asked.

'Don't know. Maybe he wants to hang out.' Scarlett giggled.

'How can you hang out with someone who doesn't say anything? I mean, that's what hanging out is. That's literally *all* it is. You hang out and talk to each other.'

'Yeah, I suppose,' said Scarlett.

'That's probably why he hasn't got any friends,' said Tiffany. 'I mean, you can't be friends with someone who can't talk, can you?'

The whole conversation was beyond horrible but that one hit me hard. A square punch to my chest. I was finding it difficult to breathe. I couldn't stop listening, even though it was causing me actual, physical pain.

'I don't really notice him, to be honest,' said Scarlett, 'You know, because he's so quiet. I forget he's there. But just before you came to Lakeside, Theo had his birthday and he invited the whole class to *RollerCentral* – that roller-disco place?'

Oh no – please don't tell her about Theo's party.

'Oh yeah,' said Tiffany. 'It's cool there.'

'The whole class goes to Theo's party, even Leo, but he totally freaks out. He doesn't skate at all. Can't even get his boots on. His big brother has to come and get him and take him home.'

'What do you mean, freaks out?'

'He freezes solid, like a statue. Can't move at all. He made this funny groaning sound in his throat. It was beyond weird.'

'I'm staying away from him,' Tiffany said, decisively and the conversation was over.

I was left reeling. It would not be different with Tiffany. I knew then that I would never have a real friend; it was impossible. I would manage to stay unnoticed, hide myself and my pain, then and forever afterwards too.

Richa does her dues and stays for the full half an hour, but I know she can't wait to get home. After Richa leaves, Ryan comes to sit next to me and we play Sonic together for a minute or two without saying anything. I know he wants to talk and here's the thing, I know I'll be able to talk back. I don't make the rules about my SM; I just have to obey them.

'Richa seems cool,' is Ryan's opener. 'Patchy is properly into her.'

'Yeah,' I say, eyes on the screen.

'Dogs are a good judge of character.'

'I know,' I say and there's a pull of longing for a friend so hard it hurts my chest.

'You'll need to explain,' Ryan says at last. 'People will always want to know why.'

'There is no why,' I say, like I have a thousand times before.

'No, but Richa needs to know that you're cool too. You're just a silent kinda cool.'

I smile at that, because I want to believe my brother. I want to think that I'm cool, but in a different, quiet way. 'How?' I ask him.

'Please tell me you're not taking advice from Ryan?' Brianne is watching our game from the living-room doorway. Her long, blonde hair is now bone dry, all the moisture sucked up by the heatwave.

'Butt out, Brianne,' says Ryan, not taking his eyes off the screen. 'Besides, you practically had the girl running for the hills with all your mud pie and domino talk.'

'Hah,' says Brianne, 'you missed it, you'll have to go back now.'

'Your fault for distracting me,' Ryan says, backtracking his player a level down.

'Why don't you write it down?' suggests Brianne to me. 'You could put it in a letter, explain how it works so that Richa understands.'

'That's actually not a bad plan, Sis,' agrees Ryan and I'm amazed. Ryan never agrees with anything Brianne suggests.

I think about Brianne's idea as I play. I don't want Richa to find out about my SM the same way Tiffany did. It needs to be my words so that she understands what it's like for me. Neither of us have phones, so I can't text her; not that it would work by text. The letter idea might be the answer, but I need to get it exactly right.

4

Dear Richa,

It's a bit odd to write Dear Richa, but all letters start that way.

Because you're my neighbour and you'll be going to my school, you should probably know why I don't talk.

The most important thing to tell you is: <u>I want to talk, but I can't talk.</u>

They call it Selective Mutism, or SM. I

hate that name. I wish I didn't have it, but I do.

My vocal cords and everything work. I talk at home, almost as much as Brianne and Ryan do, but my voice sounds loud to me when it comes out and I don't like it.

I don't know why I can't talk when I'm not at home. There are lots of things that don't make sense and are difficult to explain.

I don't remember a time before SM, but Mum says it began when I started school. I can read and write really well and that's sort of taken over my talking, replacing it.

When I try to speak to someone who isn't family the words get stuck. If feels as if my throat is too tight, like someone is squeezing it.

It can hurt.

Panic and worry and horrible thoughts swirl around inside me. Sometimes I can hear the words I want to say getting louder and mixing together inside my head with nasty thoughts.

Sometimes the SM is like a bully saying

hurtful things to me: I'm stupid or useless, and the more I try to beat the bully and push out the words, the worse it gets.

My body can get stuck.

When I freeze I feel horrible, worrying about everyone watching and thinking I'm a freak. It's better not to be seen at all. The worst thing for me is everybody staring.

One day I will beat my SM.

I can dance, I'm a good dancer, and even though at the moment because of my SM I can't dance in front of an audience, one day I want to perform in The Lion King. That's why I really liked it when you said my hair was like a lion's mane.

Don't worry – I know that nobody can be friends with someone who can't talk. I understand if I don't see you again. I just wanted to try and explain.

Bye.

Leo

(the trampoline boy from next door).

This letter is my ninth or tenth try. Our recycling bin has lots of ripped up or scribbled out attempts. It took ages, hours of embarrassing effort that felt pointless at times. I hate the fact it's not perfect, but I can't keep starting over because it's tying my stomach up in knots.

I leave the letter folded under my pillow most of the weekend, then I show it to Ryan. He cuffs me on the shoulder after reading it and says, 'That'll do the trick, Bruv. Nice one.'

To be extra safe, I show it to Brianne. Her eyes go all gooey when she reads it. When she says, 'Perfect' to me, her voice cracks.

After that I put it into one of Mum's fancy envelopes that she uses for important letters. I lick it, taking in the lovely new paper smell and stick it down. Then I write RICHA on the front and, because I can't risk anyone catching me, Brianne is the one who posts it through next door's letter box.

After that I worry and worry about what I've done, but it's too late by then to change it.

5

Monday morning comes and Brianne walks me through the dry heat for my first day at Just Jive. In my backpack, which is already starting to stick to me, are:

1. My soft dance trainers.
2. My *Gaggle Gangs* lunch box (no, I'm not getting too old for *Gaggle Gangs*).
3. My matching juice bottle.
4. My sweat towel.

5. The payment and note for my dance teacher, Mrs Delaware. ('Call me Felicity, my dear, everybody does.')
6. My notebook and pen for when I need to speak but can't.

Brianne is talking to me and I'm darting around, trying to stay in the shade and not be spotted by strangers as much as possible. It's still only early, too early to be out of bed in the summer holidays, and the temperature is already up to notch five of ten on my imaginary heat scale.

'She's probably never met anyone with SM before,' Brianne says, her flip-flops slip-slapping against her heels. It's a nice noise, comforting. I use it to steady myself against the worry of Richa's silence since my letter was posted.

'I'm sure she'll come over when she's had a chance to think about it. She's probably been doing loads of unpacking and organising.' Brianne pushes her big, owl-like sunglasses up her nose. 'I hope the letter didn't get lost somewhere.'

A big bus with a concertina middle comes by. There are six people on our side. Only one of them isn't staring or prodding at their phone: a bored-looking woman with droopy cheeks and a blotchy, beetroot face. She catches my eye and I look quickly away. The bus roars on, leaving a trail of stinking exhaust fumes that mix with the hot air.

We have to wait for the green man and there's no shade. The sun is right on top of us glaring down angrily. I can almost smell my brains cooking.

Beep, beep, beep.

Saved!

'Anyway, you did the right thing, telling her.' Brianne steps off the kerb and her skirt floats out behind her, waving me to follow. 'I wonder who'll be at Just Jive this year?' My sister walks fast and I'm trotting to keep up. 'Anton, that cute little boy with the dimples and the tap shoes, I bet he's doing it again.' Brianne scoops her hair up off her face, securing it into a ponytail. All the bangles on her arms tinkle and her thumb rings glisten in the sun like treasure.

When we reach the dance school, Brianne strides into the revolving door. There's only room for one on each side, so I wait for my turn then duck in. I'm tempted to go all the way round to be back outside. I could take off for home and not face the unknown newbies, but I force myself inside. Another test. There are always tests and rules with my SM.

The building is an old hotel, shabby and crumbling like a haunted house, but the sunshine floodlights everything, stopping it from ever looking scary.

As soon as we're inside we suffer a temporary blindness, going into the gloom from the bright dazzle of the heatwave. But I've been coming for dance lessons here once a week for the last three years, I could find my way blindfolded.

A curly staircase arcs in a big, wide sweep to the right, as if waiting for someone glamorous to waltz down it. Or better still, whizz down on the banister. There's no air conditioning like there is in the mall, but the tall ceilings and fans make it cooler than outside. It's still too hot.

Brianne strides off to the ballroom on the right, pushing open the double doors. I follow at a trot and, once I'm inside, take a lungful of the familiar, comforting dance smells – plimsols and lavender. Then I spot Richa. She's standing alongside her very pregnant mum who holds Aahan's hand.

Panic rises.

My letter, my letter, my letter.

She's read all those words.

She knows.

There's no way I can look at her face, so instead I watch Richa's knees as they fold and straighten, getting closer towards us. Aahan's little three-year-old legs are trotting behind his sister and I hear him calling after her, 'Wicher, Wicher. Wait. Wicher. Wait.'

'Hello Richa,' Brianne says, all bright and breezy. 'I didn't know you were coming. We could've all walked together.'

'Hi Brianne. Hi Leo.'

'Wicher carry. Wicher peas carry. Wicher,' says Aahan. His arms are on full overhead stretch mode. A cute distraction from my internal panic.

There's a stream of Gujarati then Richa, still ignoring her baby brother, says, 'I just told Mum she won't need to walk me home.'

'OK?' Richa's mum asks Brianne.

'Of course,' says Brianne and waves a bangled arm through the air. 'I'm happy to walk them every day, if you like. Or Ryan will. You need to put your feet up.'

33

We all stare at Richa's mum's feet that poke out from under her purple sari. They're puffy and swollen in her sandals.

'Horrible,' Richa's mum says, trying to tuck them out of sight. 'This Big Baby. And so hot.'

'Come on,' Richa whispers to me, her fingers curling over my bare arm, gently tugging me away.

I hear Aahan start to cry.

Watching our feet, I'm amazed how mine move willingly. It's as if Richa has made my body shift without me being part of the decision process. As I go with her, I hear my sister's stilted conversation and Aahan's crying getting quieter.

'So bored of boring baby talk,' Richa says, leading me over to the wheeled-cloakroom benches and pegs that run in short rows in the far corner of the room. The dance smells get stronger. 'All she ever talks about is baby this, baby that.' Richa rummages in her bag, pulls out her water bottle, and takes a quick swig. 'I think everyone talking about how hot it is makes it hotter. Plus it's boring.' Richa rolls her eyes and takes another slug of water. She hangs her bag up on a peg, then sits on the bench below and takes off her sandals. How does she know the routine? It's like she's always been coming here not me. I'm shifting my weight from one foot to another, wondering what I should look at. Richa has no idea how lucky she is.

My letter, my letter, my letter.

'Take the peg next to me.' Richa turns and grips the empty peg with her left hand, fiercely guarding it from a possible swarm of takers. I relax a bit and start wriggling out of my backpack.

Richa hasn't reacted at all to my letter, or maybe this is her reaction. Maybe this is Richa's way of saying she doesn't mind, that she still wants to be friendly.

'I'm so happy there's a dance school here,' Richa chats on. 'The last place we lived was like being in the middle of a cow field and there was nothing like this.' She waves an arm about, gesturing to the makeshift room as if we were in Pineapple Studios itself. I sit down beside her and start pulling on my dance trainers.

'They are so cool,' says Richa with genuine admiration. 'Must've been a birthday present, right? Brianne told me you've just turned ten. Me too! I asked for a phone, but Mum says I'm still too young for one. Hey, next year we can have a party together. Dad says we're definitely staying put this time. No more moving and eleven is a big deal, Leo. Big deal equals big party. You can tell me who is worth inviting out of Lakeside Primary.'

Wait… Did Richa just say that she wants to have a shared birthday party with me – the boy who doesn't talk? I know there's no way I can actually *have* a birthday party but this is a total miracle! Richa has read my letter and still wants to be friends. She doesn't care about my SM. Richa will do the talking for both of us (she is the best talker I've ever known). I suddenly feel like the luckiest boy on the planet.

'Dancers, my darling dancers wherever are you all?' The tiny, Call-Me-Felicity, glides into the centre of the room. Her back ramrod straight, her yellow hair piled up on top of her head like an ice-cream sundae. I feel ridiculously pleased to see her and grin stupidly at my shoes as I finish tying up my laces. It's almost as if my dance teacher had some hand in my remarkable turn of good fortune.

We gather about her like ducklings, and she smiles and nods at each of us in turn. 'New faces. How utterly wonderful. Parents, carers, you may leave.' Call-Me-Felicity wafts her hand high in the air as if flicking away an annoying fly. 'Collection of these delectable dancers will be at four pm. Make sure you arrive a few minutes early for our end-of-day performance.' She claps her bony hands, her heavy rings clashing together. 'We shall have a delightful day of dance, despite this dreadful heat.'

Lots of the kids turn to wave and smile goodbye and I take my chance to snatch a glance about to see who is new.

Oh no, oh no, oh no. Tiffany, Scarlett and Maryam are here. This is a complete and utter disaster. My elation instantaneously bursts like a popped balloon. I need to leave right now.

Nobody from school knows about my dancing. They all just think of me as Leo the boy who doesn't talk. Dancing is my special secret.

This is a total nightmare.

I have to leave.

I have to leave now.

6

Swivelling about, I look for my sister, but Brianne has gone. Probably the first out of the door.

I'm trapped.

A big mirror makes up the far wall and I use it to sneak glances at the three girls from my class. They've not noticed me yet, too busy admiring each other's leotards and hair clips. My brain is swirling. I take a couple of calming breaths, like my speech therapist has taught me to do. In through the nose for the count of five, out for five.

Maybe they won't even remember me. It's been months since I followed Tiffany around. I'm almost invisible at school. Completely silent, hiding in shadows, staying out of sight. Perhaps they won't think that the boy who dances is the same boy who doesn't speak.

Don't look at them.

Be invisible.

Don't freeze.

My hand goes up to my hair. My big, distinctive, orange hair. Of course they'll know it's me. You can't hide hair like mine.

'What's wrong?' Richa loud-whispers at me.

I shake my head, drop my eyes to her shoes.

Just don't look, I tell myself and concentrate on breathing.

Richa is glancing about at everyone, trying to see who has upset me. 'Can you point?' she asks me. I shake my head again.

Richa can't meet them. If she does, she'll want to be their friend and not mine. Maryam, Scarlett and Tiffany would be proper friends to Richa. They can talk.

'Let's warm up everyone,' says Felicity. 'Not that we need to in this heat. Then we'll do some group routine work.' She puts on the music. 'Heatwave' by Martha and the Vandellas blares out.

'Just my little joke, folks,' Felicity says, the headset microphone raising her voice above the music. She sets off into the warm-up routine that we're all to follow.

There's no time to let the panic of the situation properly take hold. I can't think about Richa, or the girls from my class. Instead, I close my eyes for a second or two, replacing my steady breathing with the sound and feel of the music. Letting the beat and rhythm fill me pushes out the worry and panic. I open my eyes and think only about the music. My body moves for me and I start to follow the routine.

Once I'm dancing I relax. It's always been this way. There's nothing awkward about my dancing. It's the most free and natural thing I do. It's difficult to explain, but the music takes over. I imagine it's like when the pilot of an airplane switches on the autopilot and the airplane flies itself.

The routine is basic, easy to learn. Step touch, chassé, and mambo cha cha to the right, repeat to the left, with a two-step turn in between. Richa picks it up quickly. It's obvious she's danced in a class before. The two of us fall into a natural rhythm, just like we did with the trampoline shapes. I can feel my hair bouncing and the beginnings of a smile on my face and think maybe it'll be OK. If we just dance and don't try to talk, it'll all be OK.

Richa and I are near the front. There's about twenty of us all together. Scarlett, Maryam and Tiffany make up the right side of the back row. Scarlett and Maryam are struggling, and doing their best to keep up, but Tiffany is terrible. She is all elbows and knees and has no natural rhythm at all. She keeps going in the wrong direction and nearly banging into all the other kids.

Call-Me-Felicity has clocked Tiffany. Our teacher's eyes keep flicking over to her, but she doesn't miss a beat. Felicity carries on perfectly, making her moves big and calling them out over and over so that we all know which way to go.

I've seen Felicity dance; I mean really dance. When she was young, she danced on stage. She was in all the big West End shows like *Cats* and *Chicago*. One time, when the other kids kept crazing her, Felicity showed us some videos of her dancing on YouTube. I went home that night and looked her up. I typed in Felicity Delaware and watched every clip of her dancing that I could find. She's inspiring – I want to do what she's done. If I didn't have SM I know I could.

My guess is our teacher will be taken up trying to teach Tiffany the basics. I'm hoping today will be enough to stop Tiffany from coming back to dance class. Football is her thing. I have no idea why she's here. I hate that Tiffany, Scarlett and Maryam are all here. They're going to spoil everything.

7

Tiffany and Scarlett are too busy concentrating to notice me but Maryam, getting more confident in her dancing, uses the mirror to check out the rest of the class. It's my hair that gives me away. I see Maryam do a double take when she sees it bouncing.

Maryam catches my eye in the mirror and the shock of it makes me stumble a move. I use a left, instead of a right foot, to step into a mambo. Doing a quickstep change, I fall back into the rhythm again, but Richa, so instep with me, notices everything. Using the mirror reflection, she clocks Maryam, who smiles shyly at Richa. Richa returns the smile, but bigger, more friendly.

This is the start of it. This is when Richa will get her real friends.

Maryam elbows Scarlett and nods over towards me and Richa. Tiffany is way too out of control to think about anything other than working out her right from her left. Two of the three girls from my class know that I'm here. I try to not let it affect my dancing, but it does – they do.

After a while, Call-Me-Felicity says, 'Nice work, dancers. Take a break.'

We gather round the pegs. Richa and I sit at the benches on one side of the room, the three girls from my class on the other.

It's obvious from the way Tiffany, Scarlett and Maryam all lean in together and glance our way, that they're talking about us, that is, when they're not taking selfies with their phones.

'You know them, don't you?' Richa says tipping her head at the whispering girls. Then she's immediately distracted by my water bottle. 'Oh my days…You like *Gaggle Gangs*?' she says, stabbing at the bottle with an outstretched finger. 'I love them!'

This is another miracle. Everyone at school, above Year Three, thinks *Gaggle Gangs* are pathetic.

'DogGirl is awesome. I want to *be* DogGirl. That thing she does when she communicates through their minds.' Richa mimics DogGirl's intense stare. It's a good impression. 'That's so cool. Did you see the one when she met the wolf? That's my total favourite episode. I've got the entire series on DVD. You should come over, or we can watch them on your PlayStation because I know you can play DVDs on Play—'

'Hey Leo.'

It's the sudden darkening of the sky. The terrible trio are here, looming over us like prophets of doom. I stare at their bare feet.

'Hello,' says Richa, casually. She's totally unfazed about being interrupted mid-*Gaggle Gangs* flow and I'm amazed all over again at her natural confidence. 'You friends of Leo's?' Richa asks them, then adds, 'Do you go to Lakeside too? I'm Richa. We've just moved to Luton. We've lived all over the place because of Dad's job. He's a drug rep.' She pauses for a tiny breath then adds, 'That makes him sound like a criminal.'

Richa laughs and I look up to see the three girls utterly spellbound. There's nothing quite like a new kid to create interest. Richa will be gone in a flash. There's no way she'll stay hanging out with me now.

'*Is* he a criminal?' Maryam asks, wide-eyed.

Richa laughs again and shakes her head.

'I'm Tiffany, that's Maryam and that's Scarlett.'

'Hello,' says Richa.

'You sound different. Are you from the north?' asks Scarlett.

'All over really, but yeah, born in Sheffield,' says Richa.

'We know Leo from school,' explains Tiffany, but she doesn't even glance my way. 'Didn't know he could dance though. It's not fair. You can both do it. You can all do it. Everyone can do it except me.' Tiffany tries to shrug to show that she's not bothered, but I can tell from the gritty sound of her voice and the way she bunches up her fists that she really is bothered.

There's a rush of all kinds of conflicting thoughts. I was ready to hate them all for being here and spoiling everything. I should be glad that Tiffany doesn't like dancing, because she'll probably leave. But it's not that simple. To me, dancing is brilliant and I don't like knowing that Tiffany doesn't get it. I want Tiffany to leave, but not because of dancing.

It's so confusing.

'You need to be at the front,' Richa explains, giving kind and solid advice. 'You can't see the teacher's feet properly hiding at the back. The closer you are to her the easier it is.'

'But then everyone will see me and I'm rubbish. I'm so rubbish.' Now Tiffany's voice catches, showing that she's getting upset and I'm even more confused. I'm better at something than someone else. I've only ever thought about how I'm the boy who can't talk and now here I am being able to do something that someone else can't do.

'You're not that bad,' Scarlett says and I sideways glance to watch her put her arm around her friend's shoulders. 'We've only just started. We can't do it either can we, Maryam?'

There's a beat before Maryam answers. 'I'm all over the place,' Maryam says, but I can tell that she knows she's a better dancer than Tiffany. Everyone is a better dancer than Tiffany. Do I feel sorry for her?

Richa rummages in her bag and, as she pulls out a packet of polos, I see my letter. The envelope has been opened. Richa has read my letter and brought it with her to Just Jive. What does that mean? The sight of it throws me further off balance.

Richa stands up and offers the mints to Tiffany.

'Thanks,' Tiffany says taking one and handing the packet back.

'Nobody is watching anybody else. We're all too busy concentrating,' Richa says, her voice soft and kind, but I've stopped worrying about Tiffany. The only thought in my head is that my letter is inside Richa's dance bag. 'You need to learn the names for each of the moves. It makes it a lot easier.'

'Yeah. What is all that mambo, cha cha stuff?' Scarlett asks.

I'm only half-listening.

'Why don't you all go and ask the teacher to explain the basics?' Richa suggests.

'Can't you teach us?' Tiffany asks Richa, crunching the mint between her teeth.

Now I'm listening.

'Yeah, you can dance really well,' says Maryam. 'It would be much better if you show us what to do.'

'You could come and dance near us,' suggests Scarlett. 'That way we can follow you.'

My heart lurches. This is it.

Richa glances at me and I look away, my eyes fixed on the corner of the letter poking out of her bag. I feel her follow my gaze. She knows what I'm looking at. There's a pause while Richa thinks. The decision is made. Richa will go and dance with the terrible trio. They'll be her friends now. She'll teach Tiffany to dance and they will dance together at the end of Just Jive in the show. I'll be watching, wishing that I could be part of it but knowing that I can't and it will be ten thousand times worse than last summer.

How could I be so close and still mess it up? Why are my only friends my dog and characters in books? Why can't I just talk, like everybody else?

'I suppose we could dance nearer the back, couldn't we Leo?' Richa says slowly.

There's a pause filled only with the heat and the thundering of my heart. Richa still wants me to be her friend. She wants all of us to be friends. I don't know why she does, or how she has landed here, but I am totally grateful for her.

'Not sure there's room for two,' says Tiffany. It's like another nasty blow from her. This time, a sharp, stinging slap across my face.

'It's a bit crowded at the back,' agrees Scarlett. Smack!

'I think all the new people are hiding there,' says Maryam, joining in.

All three of them are ganging up against me.

'Be best if it's just you, Richa,' says Tiffany. Slap!

'Even though Leo can dance, he won't be able to tell us the names of the moves, will he?' Scarlett says.

I sense them huddle tighter together. They're closing in on Richa, like a pod of killer whales diving down on a school of fish. This is the moment of truth; Richa has to choose. The truth is there for her to see: we can't all be friends together. I'm the loner. I'm the boy who can't talk.

How can you be friends with someone who can't talk? You can't. It's impossible.

The moment stretches – long and uncomfortable.

'You'd better ask the teacher for help then,' says Richa, her tone sharp and final.

She spins and sits down next to me so forcefully that a little whoosh of air lifts my lion's mane. It's a small movement; Richa has only sat beside me, not stepped onto the moon. But, to me, it feels just as monumental.

8

The first day of Just Jive goes on. When we're not all learning the routine, Richa and I stay on the opposite side of the room to Maryam, Tiffany and Scarlett. Undeterred by Richa's earlier snap, the trio still sidle over at break times to try to make friends with Richa. Tiffany tells Richa she likes her hair and Scarlett admires her leotard. Maryam tells Richa she has the perfect shoes, all soft and flat on the bottom, which is why she spins so well. Every time she gets a compliment

Richa says thank you, but she doesn't chat, all friendly and relaxed, like she did the first time she met them. They always ignore me, just like they do at school.

After a time, the three girls take Richa's advice, dancing in front of us, right next to Call-Me-Felicity. Tiffany tells Richa at lunch how much easier it makes learning and how right she was, even though Tiffany barely improves at all throughout the day.

It's off-putting knowing the three of them are there, waiting like cats by a mouse hole, ready for the right moment to pounce. I just want to dance and not think about the girls from my class. Luckily, it seems that Richa wants to do the same.

Call-Me-Felicity spends most of the day trying to get the room cooler and teach Tiffany some basic steps. Amazingly, despite not really having the proper teaching, by the end of the day the dance routine is about ready to show to the parents and carers who arrive to collect us.

As usual, I can't perform and, while everyone else dances to 'Carwash' by Rose Royce, I stand next to Ryan, watching as if I'm there to collect a dancer rather than to dance myself.

Richa is really good, easily the best in the class. A lot of the other kids are following her. Maryam and Scarlett just about manage to get through the song. They miss a few turns and kicks, but it's not a bad effort for their first try at a proper dance class.

Tiffany, on the other hand, sticks out like a sore thumb. She's clunky and stiff, totally out of sync, and a least two beats behind everyone else. Even though it makes me cringe to watch her so far out of her comfort zone, there's something completely mesmerising about it. It's amazing to think that someone who excels at football can be so monumentally bad at something else.

Tiffany's hair is wet through, bunched up in tiny coils, like noodles. The sweat is dripping off her nose and her T-shirt has huge, dark patches under her arms and down her back. Her skin glistens with sweat and her face is the picture of humiliation. She looks ready to give up on the whole thing and run away from the routine in tears.

I snatch a glance at her mum and dad who are standing close to me and Ryan. Her mum looks uncomfortable, wincing at every bad move Tiffany makes, but her dad is grinning broadly and nodding along in time to the music. Seeing him swaying his head happily from side-to-side, I think it must've been him who pushed Tiffany to come.

I know what it's like to be terrible at something, to stick out. Everyone here can see how bad Tiffany is at dancing, just like they know that I can't talk. These aren't secrets you can hide, not when you're on display.

The song finishes and the children and parents are pulled together like magnets.

'You did so good,' Tiffany's dad says. 'You'll be better tomorrow.'

'Dad, I'm terrible,' Tiffany says, her voice finally wobbling. 'I hate it. Don't make me come back.'

'You were good,' he protests. 'I'll buy you the right things.' He looks about at the other dancers. 'Those little twirly skirt things and some proper shoes.'

'No, Dad. You said I only had to do one day. I did what you wanted. I tried it out, but I hate it. I only want to play football. I don't like dancing.'

'But … but…' stutters Tiffany's dad. 'Maybe you should try gymnastics instead?'

'I don't want to do gymnastics. I want to play football.'

'Jim,' says Tiffany's mum, putting a hand on her husband's arm. 'We agreed for her to give it a go. She's done a whole day and she didn't want to come.' She turns to her daughter. 'You tried Tiffany, that's all we can ask. If it's not for you then it's not for you. Not everyone can dance like—' She turns to look at Richa who is sitting on the bench, changing into her sandals. 'Well, like that girl. She's really good.'

'Tiffany will be just as good as her,' insists her dad. 'She just needs more practice. And the right shoes.'

'Dad, if you want to get me shoes, buy me some Predator football boots. They're the boss.'

Her mum laughs. 'You can lead a horse to water, Jim…'

Jim, Tiffany's dad, sighs again. 'Alright. I know when I'm beat. Summer football camp it is then.'

Tiffany does her best turn all day, spinning round with a grin to face Maryam and Scarlett. 'You're on your own,' she calls over to them. 'Your best bet is to get that girl, Richa, to help you,' she jabs a thumb over to the benches. 'I'm out of here.'

Tiffany won't be coming back to Just Jive, but it's still not over. I know that Richa can only be a temporary friend. Maryam and Scarlett will keep trying until they eventually steal her away from me. Our friendship is something special but easily lost, like the DogGirl card from *Gaggle Gangs* Collectables. It's the rarest and I've never found one, but if I did, I bet it would fall out of my pocket.

I watch as Richa skips her way over to us, wishing I could skip towards her too, meeting her in the middle of the room. In my imagination we would dance together, no matter who was watching us, spinning around and around holding each other's hands.

'You busted some serious moves out there, girl,' Ryan tells her.

'Thank you,' says Richa, but she grins at me, not my brother.

My heart beats in my throat as I try to smile back but instead I look down at my temporary friend's feet.

9

The next morning Brianne and Richa chatter together on our walk to Just Jive. Listening to them makes me worry less about Maryam and Scarlett waiting to pounce on Richa the moment we arrive, but I do feel a bit forgotten. My sister has got lots of friends, she doesn't need mine.

'I would've brought Patchy,' says Brianne, her flip-flops slapping away on her heels, 'but it's boiling already. We can't walk him until about eight or nine at night because the hot pavements scald his paws.'

'Can I walk him with you both?' Richa asks, sidestepping in a skip to keep up with Brianne's big strides.

'If your mum says it's OK then yeah, but it's probably a bit late.'

'If Leo goes then so can I. We're the same age. It's only fair,' Richa says. She looks over her shoulder at me and smiles. I manage to smile back, because walking Patch would be more fun if Richa is there too, as long as the two of them don't talk all the time and leave me out. Brianne can sit on the bench and look at her phone while we play ball with Patch. He's excellent at fetch and only stops to have a long drink from the pond in the park.

'He's such a lovely dog. You're so lucky.'

'Might not think that if you had to clear up his hair every day. It gets everywhere.'

'Wouldn't bother me,' Richa says with a shrug. 'When I grow up I want to be DogGirl from *Gaggle Gangs*.'

'You don't like that rubbish TV show too, do you?'

'*Gaggle Gangs* is the ultimate,' says Richa. 'Isn't it Leo?'

I nod and feel better because I'd forgotten how much Brianne hates that show.

Brianne laughs. 'It's like Leo's dream friend just moved in next door.'

Richa really is a wish come true. Even if it doesn't last, I'm making the most of the time I've got. Last night we bounced on our trampolines again making each other laugh. When we got too hot and tired Richa came over. We crawled underneath my trampoline with Patchy and sucked on ice-cubes. It was double shady under there and Patch laid down between us so that we could each pet one of his ears. Richa chatted and I listened. She told me all about the last place she lived and the place before that and how she was glad that they'd stopped moving about. It was nice sitting and listening to her talking and for a while I even forgot about the letter I wrote her.

'Our mum got the dog for Lion,' Brianne tells Richa now. 'You've always been able to talk to Patch, haven't you?' my sister says to me and I nod. 'I think it's because Patch can't say anything back.'

Brianne is wrong – Patch says lots of things

back, just not with words. I can't put my sister right but I think about how people who speak can make up truth or lies and there's nothing I can do about it.

'They were puppies together,' Brianne says, and she smiles at me. 'Leo used to come downstairs to curl up next to Patch in his dog bed. So cute. Now the dog goes upstairs and lies on Leo's bed. He still does it, even in this heat.'

'You're so lucky, Leo,' says Richa. 'I'd do anything for a dog. Stupid Aahan. I'll just have to practise my DogGirl powers on Patch.' And even though it's too hot, Richa loops an arm through mine.

The feel of her skin makes my quick, little steps light. It's like we're dancing before the lesson has even begun. I really don't want Richa to be temporary.

'I'm so glad you two are friends. It was my idea for Leo to write the letter,' Brianne brags.

'Oh yeah, the letter,' says Richa and I feel her arm tense up. She looks at her feet as we walk. Why the sudden change? It can only mean something she's remembered that I wrote in the letter. I wonder if she has it in her dance bag again like she did yesterday. Why is she carrying it around?

'Am I supposed to write back?' Richa asks at last.

That can't be all she's worried about. It has to be to do with my SM, something Richa read that she's not happy about.

Brianne laughs. 'Not really. Leo sometimes uses a pad and pen at school and in public places so that he can talk but not out loud. While he's getting used to being your friend he might write things down for you that he wants to say but can't. Then he might be able to move onto whispering in your ear. That's right, isn't it Lion? Have I got that right?'

I nod and break my arm link with Richa so I can wriggle out of my backpack. We stop for a minute for me to show Richa the pad and pen Brianne is talking about. I thought Richa would be happy that there's a way I can talk to her, but she looks more worried than anything. I want to ask her what the matter is, and think about writing the question down, but Brianne is striding away as usual. Richa gives a little apologetic shrug and hurries after her, leaving me behind to cook in the morning sun.

'Come on, Lion, nearly there,' Brianne calls over her shoulder.

Adding Richa's reaction to my list of things to worry about it, I put the pad and pen away and hurry to catch up.

When we get to the dance studios, Richa revolves three full rotations in the door. Each time she passes me stood on the outside, she says, 'Come on, Leo.' Brianne waits inside. Her smile gets less wide after each turn. On the fourth circuit I jump in even though Richa is still turning the door. She squeal-laughs, as if she has just squirted me with a water pistol and I've done it back, and pushes the door even faster.

'Don't break it,' yells Brianne on the sixth turn, but we're laughing so much and the door is whooshing noisily around making it hard to hear her. Then I see Scarlett arriving with her mum and suddenly it's not funny anymore. I duck out of the door to stand close to my sister.

'Aw, Leo, why did you stop?' Richa says, 'We'd almost created a vortex.'

'Nice use of physics terminology, Richa,' says Brianne. Richa stares blankly at her.

Brianne sighs, 'Never mind. Come on.' She strides off towards the studios.

Richa starts to follow my sister but then Scarlett is suddenly there, with her mum, standing right in front of us.

'Hello Richa,' Scarlett says, completely ignoring me.

'Richa, that's a nice name,' purrs Scarlett's mum, also completely ignoring me. She's wearing a heavy-smelling perfume. It fills the air around us all with its sickly sweetness. 'You dance really well. I saw you yesterday.'

'Thanks,' says Richa. 'But Leo is better.'

Richa smiles at me and I'm grateful for her all over again.

I feel Scarlett's mum's eyes glance at me, but she doesn't say anything. She knows I won't be able to talk back so there's no point. Like Scarlett, all she cares about is Richa.

'Scarlett tells me you're starting at Lakeside in September?'

Richa's face falls. A sharp, dramatic change. She does a quick little nod.

'Might be a good idea to dance with Scarlett and Maryam today then?'

Richa shrugs and I shuffle my feet about, fighting the urge to run away.

'Be good to make some other schoolfriends. Don't you think?' Scarlett's mum pushes.

This means friends who can talk. Friends who aren't me.

Richa opens her mouth but for once she has nothing to say.

Scarlett's mum seems confident she has made her point. She waves goodbye, blows a kiss to her daughter and floats back out into the heatwave, leaving her perfume behind like the bus' exhaust fumes yesterday. I watch her through the glass putting her sunglasses on and decide that I don't like her very much.

'Come on, let's go find Maryam,' Scarlett says, trying to take hold of Richa's hand.

Richa snatches her hand back. 'I told you yesterday,' Richa says firmly. 'I'm dancing with Leo. Either we all dance together, or you and Maryam are on your own.'

'Suit yourself,' Scarlett says and she turns so sharply to storm off that her ponytail flicks over her shoulder.

We follow slowly behind and part of me wants

to ask Richa if she's sure. Being friends with Scarlett and Maryam would be a lot easier than with a boy who can't talk. But there's a bigger part of me that's glad I can't ask her. It feels like our temporary friendship has just been extended.

10

The second day at Just Jive goes by faster than the first. After the initial secretive whispering and finger pointing, Scarlett and Maryam seem to accept that Richa won't be abandoning me to dance with them. We stay on opposite sides of the room, sticking to our pegs like homing pigeons. This time the girls don't sidle over at break times and there aren't any more compliments. The selfies have stopped too.

If Richa notices the high chin snubs and hair

flicks she doesn't say anything. Instead, she tells me again how she wants a phone and talks about the world's ultimate dance moves. She chats about *Gaggle Gangs* and the best things to keep in a lunch box that don't turn too sweaty and nasty to eat. Strawberries and bananas are in the No Go Zone. Frozen Zubes are ranked highest because they keep your lunch – even cheese sandwiches – cool and when you come to eat them they've melted into a delicious cold yoghurt drink.

I could listen to Richa chatting forever and not get bored. She is the best talker I've ever known and never runs out of interesting things to say. Plus, she puts crisps inside her cheese sandwiches, the same as me. Cheese and onion flavour crisps work just as well as ready salted. That's something new I've discovered from Richa today. Who knew?

When we're not eating, or taking a break, we're dancing. It really is one of the best days ever. Even when Brianne and all the others turn up to for the end-of-day performance and I watch again, I still feel happy. Maryam and Scarlett being at Just Jive isn't spoiling it after all.

Richa dances brilliantly again and Brianne claps loudly for her when the dance finishes. As we wait for Richa to change her shoes and grab her things I steal a glance over to Scarlett and her mum. Maryam and her mum have joined them. The group of four are talking softly and nodding in my direction. Brianne spots them.

'Want me to deal with that situation, Lion?' she whispers to me.

I shake my head so hard my hair bounces.

Thankfully my sister lets it go, even though I know she's twitching to say something. If it was Mum she'd be storming over there, all guns blazing, but it never solves anything. People find it hard to understand why I don't talk. I can't write everyone a letter. Most people aren't worth writing letters for anyway.

'I'm starving,' Richa says when she joins us.

'Let's go to the chippy then,' says Brianne. 'I think Mum's working.' She strides away, ignoring the mums and we trot behind her like lambs.

The smell of the fried food hits us as soon as we walk in. Mum is wearing the green fish and chip shop uniform. It has a smiling fish on the chest and the speech bubble says: 'Here to Help!' It's a nice outfit, but if I was a fish in a chip shop I definitely wouldn't be smiling.

If we thought it was hot outside it's nothing to being near the fryers. Poor Mum looks redder than the beetroot woman I saw on the bus yesterday morning, but she grins when she sees us.

'Hello, hello. How was day two of dancing?' Mum does a pretend waltz with herself behind the counter.

'You should see Richa move,' says Brianne. 'Belongs on *Strictly*.'

'Really?' says Mum. 'Aw, I'd love to see you two dance together.' She does the waltz again, her head tilted to one side.

'We danced together all day yesterday and today,' says Richa. 'Leo didn't want to do the performance at the end, but he's really good. It would've been loads better if you were in it, Leo.' Richa says the last bit to me and I catch Mum and Brianne share a gooey look, like when they see me talking to Patchy.

'Maybe you can do a routine at home for us to watch?' suggests Mum. 'Alright with just me and Ryan and Brianne watching, isn't it?'

I nod. When I think about how pathetic that sounds, the dizzying heights of *Lion King* at the West End seems totally unachievable.

'What about your dad?' Richa asks me, 'Won't he want to watch too?'

Worry rushes inside me. Talk of dads is not good in my experience. Mum's reaction is unpredictable.

Luckily Mum keeps calm and just says, 'No dads around. Brianne and Ryan see their dad now and then, but Leo's dad, well, the less said about him the better.' She picks up the tongs and points them at Richa. 'Your dad could watch, though, and your mum and little Aahan. He's a cutie, isn't he?'

'No,' snaps Richa.

Mum and Brianne laugh.

'He can't come anyway. He has allergies. Patch

will make him sneeze and his nose will run. His eyes go really red and puffy.'

'Poor little boy,' says Mum and dabs at the sweat on her face with a handkerchief.

'He's not a poor little boy. He's a pain.'

'Well, we like him,' says Mum, still dabbing. 'We like all of you. Couldn't have asked for better neighbours.' Mum tucks the handkerchief away in her uniform pocket and turns over a piece of battered cod that sits on its own under the lamps. 'You never know who is going to move in, do you? But you're all a Godsend, straight up. Your mum even brought some samosas round this morning. De-lic-ious. Better than the ones off the market.'

'She must like you,' says Richa, peering at the unnatural-looking saveloys that turn slowly. 'She doesn't give them to just anybody.'

'I think she was pleased she doesn't have to walk up to the dance studios every day in the heat,' Mum says. 'Not been a soul in here for hours, I can tell you. Still too hot to pop down the chippy. Even on Friday night it was dead.'

'Everyone is eating sushi in the park,' Brianne says.

'I love sushi,' says Richa.

I love sushi too! Richa just keeps on getting better and better.

'We'll be your customers then,' says Brianne, grabbing a bottle of chilled water from the fridge.

'I knock off at five. I'll bring some freebies. Can you wait until then?'

'We can wait, can't we, kids?' Brianne says and hands Mum some coins for the water.

I smile because this means that Richa will be staying for tea.

11

When we get back to our street, Richa hands her dance bag over to me and runs home to check with her mum that she can stay for tea. She comes straight round to our house with a gigantic, 'YES!' and Patchy goes crazy when he sees her.

Richa asks for a doggy-brush so she can comb out all his fur clumps. As Richa works through his coat, Patch goes into a dream-like coma. A pile of mainly brown fluffy fur builds up next to my dog, getting bigger each time Richa cleans out the brush. I busy myself setting up a domino fall, keeping it a little distance away from the dog-grooming session to avoid a premature kick-off.

'It was even better today,' says Richa and I nod. 'I felt sorry for that Tiffany girl yesterday. She was so bad.'

Patchy does a doggy sigh of happiness, as if every word Richa speaks is the unquestionable truth. Richa won't have to wait until she's a grown up to be DogGirl – Patch is her first canine follower.

'Those girls are all from Lakeside Primary too, then? They in your class?'

I nod again.

'They weren't very nice to you. Nor were their mums,' Richa says quietly.

Slowly, I add another domino to the line, keeping my gaze on them instead of Richa.

'Is it because you won't talk?'

That hurts, and before I can stop myself, I look up at her sharply. How can she ask that after reading my letter? She should know that's one of the worst things to say to me. The most hurtful. I wrote it in big letters. I even underlined it: **I want to talk, but I can't talk**.

I can tell from Richa's face that she knows she's said the wrong thing, but she doesn't know how to make it right. She puts the brush down and twists round so she's facing me properly. Noticing the grooming has stopped without his say-so, Patch rolls off his back and onto his side. His nose hits the fur pile and he immediately launches into a comedy doggy sneezing fit. The noise breaks the tension between us.

Richa slowly strokes his head to calm him. 'It's like it should be a secret, but it can't be.' Her voice is soft and her face is difficult to read. She looks serious, maybe even a little bit scared.

I stop doing what I'm doing and watch her. Richa moves away from petting Patch and picks up her bag. Feeling around inside, she pulls out the letter I wrote to her. She still has it with her. What does that mean?

'Your secret has to be told. You can't hide it, Leo.' Richa says, still very softly, getting closer to me, the letter in her hand. 'Anyone who meets you, knows almost straight away that you can't talk, but I have a different kind of secret.' She is close enough to touch now and she stops, gently tapping the envelope into her other, open, hand.

She looks up at me, her face so close that if I leaned forward we would touch noses. Her eyes have tiny hazel flecks in them, right near her pupils.

'One I can't tell anyone.'

There's a pause. I'm desperate to know what Richa's secret is.

'Except you. I'm going to tell you, Leo.'

This is huge and I remind myself to keep breathing.

'I can tell you my secret, Leo, because you can't speak. You can't tell anyone can you?'

I shake my head.

'I know I can trust you and I have to say it. It feels too heavy.'

I watch, entranced, as Richa slowly opens up my letter, spreading it out on her bent knees that fold between us.

'I can't read,' Richa says simply. Her eyes are on my words in the letter, the words that I wanted to say to her. 'I can't read or write.'

She looks up at me and I meet her eye. And I can look at her, really look at her.

She's ashamed. I can see it in her face, in her eyes. I know because it's how I feel about not being able to talk. The shame is all over her, pouring off her hair, and her shoulders, and her skin.

Her lower lip wobbles. 'Nobody knows, Leo. I pretend that I can, but I can't and it's getting worse. It's getting harder to lie about it. I don't know what to do.'

She takes in a shuddery breath and I wish I could tell her that it's fine, that she can trust me, that she can tell me anything.

Richa takes a few more breaths and I can see that she's trying to find a way to gather the right words.

It's unbelievable to me that Richa has managed to live ten whole years and nobody knows she can't read or write. This *is* a heavy secret to carry around. I wait, and once she can, she starts to tell me her story.

'I told you already how we move around a lot?'

I nod, encouraging her to go on.

'Well, that means I'm always changing schools. By the time someone notices I've already moved on.' Richa pauses to chew at the side of her cheek. 'Dad is always working or travelling. He was born here – well in Sheffield –

same as me, and he can read and write English perfectly. He has no idea that I can't and I feel so bad for pretending to him.' Richa stares at me. Her eyes are big, wild-looking. 'Mum is from a little village outside Surat in Gujarat in India. She relies on me to speak to people: to strangers. She's got better, but she can't help me with reading or writing in English. She has no idea that I can't do it.' Her eyes start to fill up and more words tumble out in a rush. 'I don't know why I couldn't learn, but it feels horrible not keeping up. When I don't understand, I just pretend I do. I'm better at pretending than I am at learning. The gap has got so big now that I can't even try to catch up.' Her eyes are too full to hold all the tears and the left one overflows. I watch a single tear run down her cheek. 'I'm so scared about starting at Lakeside.' She picks up the letter and waves it at me. 'It's all just squiggles on a page. It doesn't mean anything.'

She looks stricken and, without thinking about what I'm doing, I put my arms around her. She leans against me, the letter crushed between us, and cries and cries and cries. Her body feels thin and frail as it shakes with her sobbing.

Richa is so strong. She seemed completely untouchable until this moment. To know her secret makes me like her even more. It's such a big thing to keep secret, and yet she's done it. How amazing that nobody else knows. How clever Richa has had to be to keep it hidden.

All that confidence: coming into my garden and finding out Patch's name; sitting on the peg bench at Just Jive to change her shoes; refusing to dance with Scarlett, Maryam and Tiffany. On the outside so bold and all the time there's this big, heavy secret buried inside.

Just like Tiffany who can't dance, but can play football, here is Richa who can do and say anything, but she can't read or write.

Nobody can do everything.

Nobody is perfect.

Patchy, fed up of being left out, noses his way between us, slowly wagging his tail. He edges in further and further still, making the letter slip to the floor. Eventually, Patch prizes us apart, until Richa isn't sobbing anymore, but laughing. That choking laughter that comes after a really good cry.

She wipes at her eyes with the back of her

hand and says, 'I feel loads better now. Lighter. Thanks, Leo. You're the best listener in the world.'

We both look down at the letter. The ink is blotched with Richa's tears. The words run into each other making it impossible for anyone to read now. Even an expert in forensics might struggle.

12

Knowing Richa's secret makes me feel special and over the next few days we get even closer. She doesn't feel temporary anymore, not now she's trusted in me. It's amazing to think that I have a real friend, that I have Richa.

Richa doesn't talk about her secret again, but as we dance, or bounce on trampolines, or go with Brianne on night-time dog walks with Patch, or watch *Gaggle Gangs*, I'm always thinking about it and how I might help.

I can look right into Richa's eyes whenever I want now. It's a big deal for me. Usually I spend a lot of time looking down at people's shoes. This is not so bad in the winter, but because of the heatwave, I'm seeing a lot of bare feet. Toes are often bulgy or disfigured and sometimes very hairy. They're not nearly as pretty to look at as eyes are. I suppose toes aren't as scary as eyes, at least, not in the same way.

Every day either Brianne or Ryan walks us in and out of Just Jive. Tiffany has still not been back, but Scarlett and Maryam have stayed. We pretty much keep out of each other's way.

Nodding and shaking my head to almost anything Richa asks me is easy now. She has learned to ask me questions that only need a yes or no answer.

Richa comes over most days after Just Jive and today she is looking around at our bookshelves in the kitchen, while I get us an ice-pop each from the freezer. I want to know what colour she likes best, so I show her the strip and she points to the blue one. I smile because I'd guessed she'd pick that one. I snip off the bubble-gum one for Richa and a strawberry one for me.

Richa says, 'I knew the red ice-pops were your favourite.'

I want to ask why, but I don't need to because she says, 'That white T-shirt you wear a lot? The one with Legsie from *Gaggle Gangs* on the front? It has a big red stain on the chest. Definitely an ice-pop stain, I thought. See, if I don't make it to becoming DogGirl, I've got a back-up plan. I can train as a police detective.'

She's right, the T-shirt does have a red ice-pop stain on it. This is not how I knew she liked blue best. Mine was a guess, but being right is more proof that we're good friends.

Richa goes back to looking at the shelves. They've just been cleaned and the furniture polish smells nice.

'You've got a lot of books in your house,' Richa says.

I nod and suck at my lolly, reading the titles as I stand alongside her.

'Is it you who does all the reading?'

I nod.

'Anyone else? Not Ryan?'

I shake my head. Ryan only reads magazines about how to make your muscles big. He works in the gym as a fitness instructor. We share a bedroom and I've seen him flex his arm muscles in the mirror and kiss them loads of times. He calls them 'my babies'.

'Your mum?'

I shake my head again. Mum sometimes takes books out of the library or borrows them from friends. Not many of the books in the house are hers. Mum says she doesn't have enough time to go to the loo, let alone read a book. She likes singing along to music. Mum has a record player and loads of records. We play records all the time. She sings and Ryan and I dance.

'Brianne, then?'

I nod. Loads of Brianne's books are about physics. She's got a whole shelf about the cosmos, but what she's really into is forces. It's why she got excited about the vortex from the revolving door.

Richa runs her finger down the hardback spine of *A History of Lise Meitner*, Brianne's heroine, and says, 'Have you got any easy ones?'

I nod again, very quickly this time, and tug at her arm to follow me. This is what I've been waiting for – a way to help with Richa's secret.

On my side of the bedroom there's three long

shelves. The bottom two are full of books. Almost half of them are picture books.

At Lakeside Primary we have a colour reading scheme. As you get better you move up though the colours and the books get more difficult. Everyone is always keen to get up to silver and gold. They can't wait to forget that purple or yellow books ever even existed. Everyone that is, except me. It's another way that I'm different from all the other kids in my class. I passed gold level in year three. I can't read out loud, because of my SM, but my reading level is tested using comprehension questions. This means I'm a 'free reader' and can choose any book from the library I want. Sometimes I choose thick books with small, difficult words, but sometimes I pick an early reader with letters as big as my fingers and bright, colourful pictures. I don't think of reading as always marching forward. To me, it's a bit like swimming. Just because you can swim up and down in the deep end, it doesn't stop you from wanting to jump around in the shallow end too.

With Richa, I scan my books, and find the one I want to share.

Brianne says everyone has a book that turns

them into a reader. They may not remember their book, but I remember mine: *Bronco*.

It's about a horse: a colt who doesn't want to do what the other colts are doing – bucking and chasing one another. Bronco wants to graze quietly by himself and think. Richa looks at the yellow cover and the picture of Bronco. She feels the book and turns it over in her hands, then opens it up.

It's an old book, written a long time ago. It has simple, black-and-white pictures and big words. Not all the words are easy, but it's a simple story. Brianne got it for me from a charity bookshop when I was very small, saying they'd told her it had come all the way from America and was very rare. Brianne used to read it to me and I followed the words. That's the way most children learn to read. The words are on one page, the picture on the other.

Richa turns the pages.

We are not most children. Richa can't ask me to read it out loud to her and she can't read it herself. Instead, we sit side by side, with Patch, quietly turning the pages and looking at the pictures.

People often rush to fill the quiet with words, but I like it. There's something gentle about the quiet; it's like the air is holding me.

As I read the familiar words inside my head I'm thinking and thinking about how we could make it work.

I want so much to help Richa to learn to read. She has given me everything and I want to give her something back. I wish I knew how.

13

It's Friday morning, which means I have been friends with Richa for nearly two whole weeks. We're over halfway through the three weeks of Just Jive. Ryan is walking us in and Richa is chatting on as usual, making us laugh. There's no concertina bus this morning but a woman runs towards us pushing a double buggy with three wheels. I can hear her feet hitting the pavement and the sound of her breathing. The two noises combine into a steady rhythm. The woman is wearing white headphones and running gear. One of her kids is a baby and the other one is about two or three years old. He is pushing against the buggy straps, like he's urging his mum to run faster. He probably wants some cool wind on his face, instead of all the heat.

'Hi Ryan,' the woman says. As she runs by, she pulls out one ear bud then waves a hand in the air at my brother.

'Hey, Janine,' says Ryan.

'Two pm for weights session, right?' The woman calls over her shoulder.

'Yep. See you then.' Ryan calls back then quickly whips out his phone. 'Totally forgot about that,' he tells us. He stops to open the voice memo app on his phone.

'What's that?' asks Richa, looking over his arm.

'This? You can record anything audio and it plays it back when you need it.'

Ryan uses the app to record a reminder to himself about the weights session with Janine and saves it, showing us how he does it.

'What's that one?' Richa asks, pointing.

'I've labelled them, so that I remember what

they all are. You can read it if you like,' offers Ryan.

'The letters are too small,' says Richa. 'What does it say?'

She's so casual about it and it makes me think of all the times she has had to cover up her secret. Ryan reads the label of the recording that Richa pointed out and laughs. 'Maybe that's not one for the ears of ten-year-olds. I'll play you this one instead.'

Ryan presses play and the noises of the gym flood out of his phone into the hot air of the morning. You can hear the tinny music and the steady tread of the running machines. There's some heavy breathing and straining and groaning noises. Then Ryan's voice blares through it, drowning out the other sounds of the gym as he talks about a workout routine for one of his clients, a man called Dirk.

My mind starts to whir with the beginnings of an idea. Maybe there is a way I can help Richa learn to read after all. If only I can get hold of a phone. I think about Maryam, Scarlett and Tiffany all taking selfies on the first day of Just Jive. It's annoying not having my own phone.

At the mention of burpees on Ryan's recording Richa giggles.

'Burpees,' she says, making herself laugh again.

'They're a killer, burpees are,' says Ryan with a straight face, stopping the recording.

'Aahan's are,' says Richa, 'especially after a pakora or two. They stink.'

The first part of Friday morning is spent on the warm-up routine as usual, but then Call-Me-Felicity drops a bombshell.

'I'm going to try something different this year,' she says, twisting her hair back up into a bright-blue banana clip. 'Instead of doing a big group performance here, like we usually do, I want to showcase individual dancers. You need to decide if you would like to do an independent dance, work in pairs, or in a small group.'

Richa catches my eye in the mirror, she's grinning. Has she forgotten that my SM means I can't perform?

'You need to choose your own music and

devise a short dance routine that incorporates the steps we have learnt over the last two weeks. All of next week we'll spend practising your dances ready for Friday's performance.

A hand goes up.

'Yes, Maryam?'

'Will there be an audience?' Maryam asks.

'Yes, and not just parents and carers, because … drum roll please, Anton.'

Anton obliges, stamping his tap shoes as quick as he can against the wooden floor.

'We have use of Luton Library Theatre – for free!'

The drum roll stops, replaced by an excited ripple of whispers. When it settles, Felicity has more to tell us.

'I'll print off some flyers and posters for you all to give out and I'll make sure it's on social media, but the more people you tell the better. There's nothing like performing to a crowd. It's a real buzz. Plus, whichever group or individual gets the biggest round of applause will be crowned the winners. They'll get the prize – a voucher to spend in *Get Dancing*.'

'I could get dance shoes like yours,' whispers

Richa. She sounds just as excited as she looks. She's definitely forgotten that there's no chance I'll be performing and there's no way to remind her.

'Now is as good a time as any,' says Felicity. 'Take some time to talk to the people you want to work with and then we'll come back and work on learning some more steps. Go, go, *vamos*.'

There's a flurry of movement as kids start to rush about, gathering allies and talking quickly and urgently with one another. It's just like at Lakeside, when we're allowed to pick our own groups. All the boys and girls separate and the most popular, or loudest kids start pulling in the strongest to be in their group.

Richa has taken hold of both my hands and is talking urgently to me. 'Not being big-headed, but we're definitely the best dancers here, Leo. We can easily win.' She lets go of my hands and claps her own together. She's really excited and talks in a big, breathless rush. 'We get to perform our own dance, Leo. This is brilliant! We've got a whole week to work on it too. I'm just thinking whether we should go for something classic, you know, like a proper couple dance. Maybe a tango? Or if we should think of something more modern? Waltzing round together might make your mum get all soppy, but will we get the applause? It's the applause we need. That's what is going to win us that voucher.'

'Hi Richa. Hi Leo.'

Maryam and Scarlett have sidled their way to stand beside us. This cannot be good. I notice that their matching purple hair clips are looking a bit less sparkly than they did at the start of Just Jive.

'Can we be with you two?' Scarlett asks. She says two, but she's only looking at Richa.

'Well…' Richa begins, she side-glances at me and I let my gaze drop to Maryam and Scarlett's twenty bare toes. Toes with bright-pink painted toenails. They probably painted each other's, because that's what good friends do.

'It's just that Leo and I were thinking of doing a partner dance and…' Richa trails off. She's on her own with no help from me and she knows it, even if she can't read my letter.

'But what if Leo won't perform?' Maryam asks simply.

I can feel all their eyes on me and it's horrible, like being a zoo animal.

The silence is long, hot and uncomfortable. I catch the faint scent of Scarlett's mum's heavy perfume. It must've rubbed off onto her daughter.

'If we work out a routine with all four of us in it,' Scarlett starts out, 'then, if Leo won't do it when the time comes, we can all still dance.' She points to herself, Maryam and Richa in turn. 'It could work in a group of three or four. But if it's just the two of you and Leo won't dance then you won't be able to perform on your own – will you?'

Even though it annoys me that Scarlett says 'won't' and not 'can't' as if I have choice about my SM, what she says makes a lot of sense. I'm less than keen about dancing with her and Maryam, but there's no point making a routine with just Richa that she can't do on her own. The truth is I'll never be able to perform. I know it, but Richa seems to have forgotten or maybe she doesn't really understand. She should understand. I feel a bit angry that she still doesn't seem to get it.

'I might,' says Richa, and from the reflection, I see her lifting her chin in the air. 'Depends on the routine. Besides, Leo is by far the best dancer in this whole class. And if Leo wants to be in *Lion King* one day, then he has to start somewhere, doesn't he?'

My head shoots up. How did she know that? I wrote it in the letter, but she can't read.

Scarlett and Maryam stifle laughter.

'What?' asks Richa. 'I believe in Leo.'

Maryam slides her eyes over to me and I look at her feet again. 'I'm not being nasty or anything, but Leo, well, he's like really, really shy and even though he can dance, he won't dance in front of people.'

This is another lie that I can't correct. I don't have shyness, I have Selective Mutism.

'He dances in front of us every day,' reasons Richa.

'But he never dances when the grown-ups come to collect, does he?' interjects Scarlett.

Richa has no answer for that.

There's a rush of feelings again. On one hand, it's horrible to listen to them all talking about me as if I'm not there. But on the other hand, Richa just told them she believes in me. She thinks that I can do it.

Only I can't do it and she should know that.

I wish the ground would open up to swallow me whole and waves of humiliation are sweeping over me. I watch the pink painted toenails, telling myself it's just another SM test and it will be over soon.

'Maybe just have a think about it?' Maryam suggests. 'Come on, Scarlett.'

We watch their backs as they walk over to the peg benches. Richa grabs the top part of my arms, spinning me to face her. I make myself look up into her face.

'We're not dancing with them. You have to perform with me, Leo. I know you can do it. Ryan and Brianne have both told me about your *Lion King* dream. Just think about this being one step closer to that West End stage. It's not just about getting that voucher. I want to dance with you on a proper stage with a proper audience. I want this more than anything, Leo. You've got a whole week to get used to the idea. You're my friend, so I know you'll do your best to do it.'

14

After Just Jive that night I'm bouncing on my trampoline, trying to think of a way to make my phone recording idea work, when Richa appears. Her head pops up and down the other side of the fence, just like on the first day I met her.

'Hey Leo,' she says.

She's trying not to ask. She lasts three bounces. 'Have you decided yet?'

I shake my head. Richa spent all day talking about different ideas but we can't even decide what type of dance to do for our routine, let alone what song to use. There's so much choice!

'Salsa?' Richa asks on her next bounce.

I shrug – this is a new addition to the head nods and shakes. Major progress.

'Jazz?'

I do jazz hands when I'm at my highest bounce point and Richa laughs.

'Merengue?'

I nod at that one. Merengue is one of my favourites. I like all the twisting. I'm playing along. I know I won't be able to perform, but I love all the preparation; deciding on the dance; going through Mum's records to pick the music. There's no way to tell Richa, but she's my friend, she'll understand. I'll be able to perform here, at home, to family. She'll have to be happy with that. She can save up her pocket money or ask for the dance shoes for Christmas, whatever comes first. It seems funny thinking about Christmas in the middle of a blazing hot heatwave.

'Nah,' Richa says. 'Merengue is boring.'

Lots of things are boring to Richa.

'Street? What about some hip-hop?'

I shake my head. We've not been learning street dance at all this week.

'Jive – got to be jive, that's the name of the class. We'll get extra cheers for that.'

What I really want her to say is disco. Even though we won't be performing it for real, disco is the most fun to dance and the music is brilliant. Earth, Wind and Fire – Mum has a few of their records – their songs are the best. The clothes are hilarious! We can start to work out the routine over the weekend, even if the heatwave tries to stop us. Then we'll be ahead of all the other dancers in the class.

To steer her in the right direction I start bouncing some disco moves. I jump high and roll my arms round one another in the 'eggbeater'. I keep doing it for a few bounces until Richa catches on and copies. Then I do 'hitching a ride' when you head pop with your thumb out, jerking it in time to your head, over one shoulder and then the other. Richa copies.

'Disco!' She says and does the classic Travolta move – one arm pointing right up in an angle, hips jutting the other way. I copy and we bounce in sync for a while doing more disco moves. It's the best!

My brother appears. He's wearing a crispy new, light-blue shirt and trainers so white you need sunglasses to look at them. 'Hey Lion, I'm off,' he says, not looking up from his phone.

'Wondered what the smell was,' Richa shouts.

'Ha ha,' says Ryan.

Richa's joke is not far off the truth because he smells of that stuff he's always spraying on himself. It pulses off him like the heatwaves coming off the pavement.

'You actually do smell,' says Richa. 'Even from all the way over here I can still smell it. You smell sweet, like Gol Papdi.'

'Thanks – I think,' says Ryan, and Richa laughs.

'This phone is rubbish,' says Ryan still prodding away at the screen.

'You need an upgrade,' Richa advises.

'Thanks, oh wise one,' Ryan says, looking up to grin at me.

'He's going on a date,' Richa says with a knowing look.

But I'm not listening because I'm thinking about the phone. Richa is onto something – if I can get Ryan to upgrade and give me his old phone, then I can help with her reading for definite.

'You stink,' Brianne tells Ryan as she comes outside.

'I love you too, Sis.' Ryan blows her a kiss. 'Don't wait up, kiddie-winks.'

'You'll be back by ten, I guarantee it,' Brianne calls over her shoulder, then turns to us as we bounce. 'No girl will be able to stomach that stench for longer than an hour or so.'

'He smells nice,' says Richa and does a backwards somersault.

'I'd rather sniff the dog,' says Brianne. 'Talking of which, I'm taking Patch out in ten minutes. You two want to come?'

'Yeah!' shouts Richa and leaps off the trampoline. Richa will never get bored of Patch.

Later, in the middle of the night, I wake up hotter than is humanly possible. Patch is a smelly, boiling-hot dog blanket spread out on top of me. My wriggling finally wakes him and he yawns a big dog-food breath yawn right into my face.

'Get off, Patch,' I tell him.

Very slowly he stretches his way off my bed, leaving one defiant back paw behind, to show how much I have inconvenienced him by waking up.

It's dark, really dark.

I'd almost forgotten about the dark. Usually there's nothing but endless sunshine, zapping the water out of the world. The dark is suddenly something exciting and unexplored.

Our curtains aren't drawn all the way across and a shaft of moonlight spills into our bedroom. It shows my brother, sprawled on top of the covers on his bed, face-down. I didn't hear him come in and, as I look at him sleeping, I wonder what's woken me up now. Glancing at the clock, I see it's just gone three in the morning.

One of my brother's arms dangles off the bed. He's wearing nothing apart from his navy pants which have ATHLETE written in capital letters round the white elastic top. His phone is charging next to him, a soft light flicking on and off.

The phone that I need to make mine.

I'm suddenly very awake and filled with an urgent mission. Taking a piece of scrap paper and a marker pen I write a note in capital letters for Ryan. Simple and to the point, it reads: UPGRADE YOUR PHONE. GIVE YOUR OLD ONE TO ME (LION). I leave it on the carpet, right where his feet will go when he wakes up. Then I unplug Ryan's phone and take a snapshot of my note. My brother doesn't make a sound, even when the flash goes off. I save the photo as his wallpaper for good measure. Finally I grab the copy of *Bronco* and, taking Ryan's phone with me, head downstairs. Patchy, properly awake too now, pads after me.

The kitchen is lovely and cool.

Human beings should all become nocturnal during a heatwave, I decide.

It's blissful being out of that horrible, hot, tight feeling.

Wind and rain feel very far away and snow is practically imaginary. The cool of the night is like a tiny slice of heaven.

I pour myself a glass of milk. Sitting at the kitchen table, I spread out the book and get Ryan's phone ready. After taking a long drink, I clear my throat, press record on voice memo and start my idea.

15

Ryan must've come in really late, way past the ten pm prediction Brianne made, because he doesn't wake up the next morning. This is good for me because it means I can share with Richa what I created in the middle of the night.

Richa comes round straight after breakfast, keen to work on our disco routine.

On the dog walk yesterday we agreed that we would dance to 'Disco Inferno' by The Trammps. Brianne and Richa started singing it as we walked round the park. Patchy got so excited he started barking. It was pretty funny – like he was joining in.

'Hey Leo.' Richa bounds up our back garden with Patch jumping with delight by her side. 'Is Brianne really going to help us with costumes? Did she mean it?'

I nod, and wave for her to come into the house. Brianne had been clear with Richa, I heard what she said even though she was supposed to be whispering.

'Don't be upset if Leo can't perform, OK? I'll make the costumes but he will probably only do the dance at home to family.'

Richa had nodded and they both looked across at me. I pretended that I hadn't heard them and threw the ball for Patchy.

'What you got there?' Richa asks me, coming into the kitchen and sitting down next to me at the table. 'Is that Ryan's phone?'

I nod and show her the set of headphones and the copy of *Bronco*.

Richa watches me enter the passcode. The less than subtle replacement wallpaper I made instantly appears. Richa has no idea what it says so she doesn't mention it. But when she sees me open up the voice memo app on Ryan's phone, her face stretches with shock. 'You're never going to play me the forbidden recording, are you? The one...' she mimics my brother's voice quite accurately, '...not for the ears of ten year olds?'

I shake my head, but I'm smiling.

This is the moment and I have to concentrate – to force myself to go on.

I plug in the headphones, put one in my right ear and gesture for Richa to put the other in her left ear. She does, then I press play on the recording I made in the middle of the night.

I really don't want to listen to my voice and especially not with Richa hearing it too, but there's no other way to do this. I can feel the SM starting to build; a flutter of anxiety, like butterflies in my chest, my heart beating faster, a tightening around my throat.

This is the first time Richa has ever heard how I sound. It's mortifying but it's worth it – she's worth it. I try my best to swallow the feelings down and concentrate on my breathing to steady myself.

My voice begins, wobbly and small: *The Story*

of Bronco by Darlene Day. Drawings by Rory Dawson.

As my voice plays from Ryan's phone, down the wire and into our ears, I run my finger under each word printed on the yellow cover of the book. Then I open the book. My words come again: *The classic story of the young stallion who would rather think than buck.* Again, I run my finger under the words of the introduction and then turn to the first page. Concentrating on the task is helping to control the feelings. I'm adjusting to it. I can do this.

The O in 'once' is huge, taking up the whole left corner of the first page. All my recording says is: *Once upon a time in Texas.* Each word is spoken slowly. There's a big pause, giving Richa time to look at the drawing of the tall American buildings on the hill and the valley with the horses below. I turn the page again and follow the words that we hear with my finger. *There was once a young colt and his name was Bronco.* The picture is of a foal, far away from the other horses grazing peacefully. Richa glances up at me, her face filled with grin. A grin that says, 'wow'. Her eyes snap back to the book, hungry for more.

I turn the page again. *All the other foals he lived with would buck and jump and race one another.*

And so we go on, slowly, carefully, page by page, until we get to the very last page of the book with the picture of Bronco winking and the words: *THE END.*

The recording comes to a stop.

Richa is beaming, I mean really smiling and it's the best kind of catching because it makes me smile too. I only truly know that I've helped her when she says, 'again'.

It only takes Richa an hour or so to learn *Bronco* off by heart. She says her favourite word is 'lonesome' or maybe, 'rodeo' – although 'butt' is probably more useful.

We return Ryan's phone to charge, next to my note and my brother hasn't moved. He doesn't even stir when Patchy licks his bare thigh and Richa giggles.

The rest of Saturday morning is spent in the library. Brianne is really pleased because it's one of the few places in Luton, other than the mall (which Brianne calls, 'A Plastic Throw-Up,' but I quite like), that has air conditioning. Brianne drops us in the children's library, that smells of new books and freshly cleaned carpets, then goes up a floor to study.

Richa asks to join the library. Luckily, the librarian fills in everything on the computer for her, and Richa gets a brand-new library card. Richa asks about the audio books. If I do get Ryan's phone we'll have loads of reading material, because there's an app you can download to borrow audio books. For now, there are a few books in the library that come with CDs. Richa has an old CD player of her dad's so that's where we'll start.

It's amazing to see how excited Richa is about learning to read. She flicks through loads of books and when she sees a word she remembers learning from *Bronco* she says it out loud, all proud.

'Years' and 'mother' and 'understanding' and 'quietly' and 'shouted'.

There's a lovely tingly feeling inside me to see my idea working. I've never helped anyone before and it feels amazing.

16

Sadly, Ryan doesn't give me his phone. Instead he throws the balled-up note at my head and says, 'Nice try, Lion.'

It's disappointing, but at least Richa has the CDs, and can follow along in the books. She tells me that learning to read is loads easier this way. Watching her, I realise that she must've always been able to read. What happens with her reading seems similar to my SM, she gets frightened about not being able to do it and the fear blocks her way.

It's brilliant to watch Richa learning new words all the time. Soon she won't have to pretend anymore, she'll just be able to do it. I hope she remembers that I helped her when it comes to me not being able to perform. I want her to know that even though I can't be the perfect friend I can still be a good friend.

We get the idea for the choreography for our dance performance from when we mirrored each other's moves on our trampolines. All the classics are in our routine. My favourite is the funky chicken and Richa likes the rolling grapevine.

Brianne makes our costumes out of a couple of bits and pieces she picks up from a charity shop. It's where Brianne gets all her clothes and she's really good at sewing and altering things to make them fit. She calls it 'bespoke fashion'. Ryan says she dresses like an old lady.

Richa has sequinned silver hot pants in an all-in-one and I've got big white flares and a sleeveless top with huge collars. My hair is already big and bouncy so I don't need a wig, but Brianne lets Richa borrow a gold and silver sparkly one that she used for a fancy-dress party ages ago. I like the idea of wearing a costume because it's like I'm pretending to be someone else completely. Someone without SM.

When the time for the dress rehearsal at the dance studios comes around, Brianne paints Richa's face with gold eyeshadow. We look brilliant and our dance is so perfectly polished that I wish all over again that I could fight my SM enough to be able to perform with Richa, even though I know it's impossible.

Everybody in the whole of Luton is coming to the evening performance apparently, and Richa is beyond excited. I'm worried that she really believes I will do this, and when I can't she'll feel so let down that she won't want to be my friend anymore. But I'm also a bit angry at her for not understanding properly and acting like she just expects me to do it.

Ryan and Brianne both come to the dance studios for the dress rehearsal on Friday afternoon. They stand away from us, at the far side of the audience. Richa's mum and Aahan are nearer to us, mainly because Aahan is fascinated by the sequins on his big sister's costume. His little, pudgy fingers keep reaching up to pick at them.

Their mum is way too pregnant to lift Aahan up to carry him, so she just leaves him to it.

'Get off, Aahan,' Richa says swatting her brother's hands away. 'Mum, Dad is definitely coming tonight, right?'

'Yes, tonight,' Richa's mum says, fanning herself with a folded-up copy of *Luton Today*. 'Dad and Leo mum have ticket. We all come tonight.'

'Good! Aahan, just leave them. They're not sweeties.' She pushes her baby brother away, but more gently this time. 'Oh look – Anton is up,' Richa says, pointing.

Anton is the only dancer going solo because he's the only one doing a tap performance.

He kicks off the dress rehearsal wearing a coat and tails, dancing the tap classic to 'Singing in the Rain'.

'Bet he's baking in that outfit,' Richa whispers to me.

I nod. It's an odd choice, especially as the

whole of Luton has dried up like a salt and vinegar chip stick in the heatwave.

'There's zero chance of rain,' Richa whispers, 'but he's not bad.'

Anton gives a really good dance performance and everybody claps and cheers for him, even Aahan, his tiny palms bashing together. I wish it was me that they were clapping for.

Scarlett and Maryam go next with what's more like a gym display than a dance routine. It's set to 'Roar' by Katy Perry. It's OK, especially considering they've only been coming to classes for three weeks, but there's no way they'll be winning the voucher.

One more group of four girls are up next, doing a jive routine to 'Summer Lovin'' from *Grease*. It's pretty good, then it's our turn.

Richa starts tugging at my arm, trying to get me into position. Even though I want to, there's no way I can do it. There must be at least thirty people watching – that's sixty staring eyes. Nobody but me and Richa dancing – there's no way I can go out there and dance with sixty eyes all staring at me. No amount of applause will make me do it. I'll freeze for sure.

'Come on, Leo,' Richa urges. 'I know it's hard, but I need you. We've done all this work and everyone is here. They're all waiting for you.'

Every single word she says makes it worse. I'm angry at her for not getting it. I shake my head and look down at the thirty pairs of feet and hairy toes all shifting uncomfortably about in the heat.

'Leo, just go out there and dance. What was the point of doing it all if you're not going to dance?'

She glances over to where Scarlett and Maryam are sniggering and whispering to each other and their mums. Richa turns back to face me and I can see her getting more and more frustrated.

I can't say or do anything, but my thoughts are loud inside my head, bouncing against one another. 'Disco Inferno' starts up. I know everyone is looking at us ... staring at me. They're all waiting and I can't move. I want it all to stop, for everyone to leave me alone.

I watch the feet shift sideways, making way for Ryan's white trainers and Brianne's flip-flops.

'It's OK,' whispers my sister into my ear. 'You don't have to do it. Nobody is going to make you.'

There's a moment of slight relief, then Richa lets go of my arm. I lift my head to watch her run, without looking back, out into the middle of the performance area. Her mum has to catch Aahan's arm as he tries to toddle after his big sister.

'Wicher,' he calls after her, a cry of desperation and longing. I know exactly how he feels but mine is more complicated, mixed up with my SM.

Richa starts the routine without me. I want to run in the opposite direction, but I can't move. Half the people there are watching me, half watch Richa. My brother stands on one side of me and my sister is on the other. Bodyguard protection from everyone's confused stares.

Richa's dancing is angry and the routine looks wrong without a partner. The song finishes and everyone claps, but it's an awkward noise made by uncomfortable people. Everything is beyond horrible.

Richa storms over, no intention of lowering her voice. 'Thanks for nothing, Leo,' she shouts, right into my face.

'Aw, Richa. Come on, mate,' reasons Ryan. 'No need to be nasty.'

'You read Lion's letter, and I did warn you this might happen when we were in the park,' says Brianne.

'You know the score,' says Ryan.

Richa glares at me harder, because she hasn't read the letter, she doesn't know the score. I'm angry with her for not understanding about my SM, but is that fair?

Richa turns and storms off. Aahan trots a little way behind his sister, with his arms up saying, 'Wicher, carry. Wicher, carry, Wicher.' Their mum gives us a sad little smile then waddles after them.

Watching the three of them go, I feel terrible, but I can't run after her. Even if I did catch up with her I couldn't say anything. This was what I was worried about and now Richa probably won't want to be my friend anymore. Tiffany's words come flooding back to me, bullying me like my SM does, 'You can't be friends with someone who can't talk, can you?'

The rehearsal goes on, but I can't stand Maryam and Scarlett's 'told you so' stares so Brianne has a quiet word with Felicity and we slip out. 'Come on,' Ryan says. 'I'll treat us to an ice cream from the kiosk in the mall on the way home.'

As soon as the glare of the heatwave hits us, we all put on our sunglasses. I'm extra hot in my white nylon outfit. It feels like punishment for not dancing with Richa, for expecting too much, for messing up our friendship.

'That's the stuff,' Ryan says when we feel the lovely cool air conditioning of the mall. It is a relief to be out of the heatwave, but I still feel miserable.

'All the electricity for air conditioning and shopping malls is why we've got this heatwave in the first place,' preaches Brianne, but she still takes the escalator to the kiosk instead of the stairs.

Ryan surprises us all by paying for all our cones – even Brianne's lemon sorbet. Richa's outburst has called a temporary truce between them. We sit in the only quiet place, at the bottom of the escalators by the drinks machine, and lick away. The air conditioning and ice cream should be making me feel better, but I can't seem to calm all my conflicting thoughts enough to enjoy it.

'I think Richa was a bit harsh on you,' says Ryan.

'Maybe I shouldn't have done the costumes. It might've made her think that you were definitely going to do it,' says Brianne. 'Plus, because you'd written it in your letter, we both did talk to her about your dream to get to the West End.'

'No way,' says Ryan. 'I'm not having that. Richa read all of that letter, she knows about the SM.'

'She's a kid herself don't forget and she's probably never met anyone else with SM before. Still, you're right. She did read that letter.'

They keep talking about the letter and it makes me feel worse about being angry with Richa for not understanding. It's putting me off my ice cream.

'That girl shouted right into his face, Brianne, in front of everyone. Out of order.'

'Yeah. That was nasty.'

I can't listen to them anymore. This isn't fair, not on me and not on Richa. Taking a deep breath, I tap on my sister's shoulder. She automatically tucks her hair behind her ear and offers it to me. This is how I can sometimes speak when we're not at home.

I whisper, 'Richa hasn't read my letter.'

Brianne straightens up and looks at me. 'What do you mean? Course she's read it, we talked about it afterwards, remember? She asked if she had to write back.'

I shake my head and Brianne lowers her head again. 'Richa can't read,' I whisper.

Brianne looks at me then at Ryan and back at me. 'Are you sure?'

I nod this time and lick my ice cream. Now she will be fair on Richa. Without reading the letter Richa can't understand what I feel inside about my SM. How can Richa know how frightening the idea of performing is if she doesn't really understand? She felt humiliated dancing on her own. I let her down, that's why she shouted at me.

'What did you say, Lion?' asks Ryan.

'He told me that Richa can't read,' says Brianne. 'She never read his letter because she can't. That's why she got angry, because she doesn't understand about his SM, not properly.'

I nod at both of them, thinking how glad I am

that I've set the record straight. Now they won't be so hard on Richa. Satisfied, I go back to my ice cream.

Brianne and Ryan have stopped eating theirs.

17

When we get home Richa is sitting on our front step, still wearing her dance costume. I'm so happy that she's there I almost rush over towards her. I thought she might never speak to me again.

We can hear Patch scratching frantically at our front door and whining to be let out to be near her.

'Mum forced me to come,' is Richa's opening statement, making it clear she's not sorry and will not apologise.

But I don't care. Richa is back!

'It's so hot out here,' she says, getting up.

'Let's go inside then before Patchy bursts his way through.' Brianne unlocks the door and there's a mad flurry of white and brown fur.

'Hello boy,' says Richa making a fuss of the dog. Patchy rushes between us all snorting and squealing as if he's not seen us for a week. Trying to get past him, we all traipse down the hallway and into the kitchen.

Brianne gets herself a glass of water and starts drinking it without bothering about ice.

'Share the love,' says Ryan.

Brianne pauses her hydration long enough to say, 'Get your own.'

Guessing the truce is off it's me who gets everyone else a drink. We all guzzle in harmony. That's how it is in the heat. You can't drink as fast as you sweat it out. Water comes before everything, even sorting out tricky friendship messes.

'Why did you shout and storm off like that?' Ryan asks Richa at last.

I wince inside at that. Ryan sounds angry at Richa and I don't like it, especially when I've told him why already.

'I stormed off because I thought you wanted to dance with me,' Richa says to me. 'We picked the song, we worked out the dance, we chose the outfits. We did all that together. I thought you wanted to do it, but you were just pretending. You were never going to even try. Those smug girls Scarlett and Maryam were laughing at me. That's why I'm angry.'

If I look at it from Richa's eyes then I can see why she would be angry.

'You need to read Leo's letter. Then you'll know about the SM,' Ryan says, gesturing with the top of his empty glass at Richa.

Why would my brother say that?

'I did read it,' Richa lies and I catch Ryan and Brianne swap a knowing glance at each other.

This is not going well and I'm so hot in this tight outfit.

'To ask Leo to perform in front of strangers is too much, even if it is dancing which he loves and is really good at,' says Brianne. 'We all went along with the costumes, but none of us really thought he would perform. Maybe here, for us, but not in front of strangers. No way.'

Richa glares at us all over the rim of her glass

as she drinks. I feel bad but I also want Richa to listen so that she understands this is about my SM, not her. I want her to remember how I've helped her with her reading.

'Do you still have Leo's letter that he wrote you?' Brianne asks and I think about the tear-stained words and wonder where Brianne is going with this.

Richa pulls her glass away, nods and swallows at the same time.

'Maybe you could go get it?'

'Why?' asks Richa.

'So that either me or Ryan can read it to you,' says Brianne. 'Then you can understand properly.'

No, no, no, no – what is Brianne doing?

'I told you! I read it already. I do understand,' Richa says. She looks panicky. 'You both told me about Leo wanting to dance in *The Lion King*. How is he ever going to do that if he can't dance in front of a few parents?'

'Don't know,' says Brianne, 'but we know enough about his SM not to try and force him to do something he isn't ready to do.'

Richa looks like a frightened, trapped rabbit.

She sips at her water, glancing from my brother to my sister and back to me. Patch goes to sit beside her but she doesn't even look at him. I get an urge to grab Richa's hand and run off with her and Patch to hide in our secret spot underneath my trampoline.

'Just go and get that letter, Richa,' says Ryan leaning back against the worktop with a sigh. 'We know that you can't read. Lion told us.'

Richa spits her water everywhere. 'You told them my secret?' she shouts at me.

This is the worst thing that could happen. Why did Ryan say that?

'Don't be angry with Lion,' says Brianne, defensively. 'He only told us because we were trying to understand.'

'How could you?' Richa says to me. 'I thought you were my friend.'

The look on her face is heart-breaking and it's only then that I realise what a terrible mistake I have made.

Richa thrusts her empty glass at me as she bursts into tears. She runs through our back door and out into our garden, Patchy close behind.

'Wait,' Brianne calls after her. 'It's nothing to be ashamed of. We can help. Wait – don't be angry, please.'

But she's gone.

It's all ruined.

I've ruined it.

I've been so stupid. Richa would've got over the performance, but she will never forgive me for telling her secret. She won't be my friend now, not after what I did. And she was the best friend ever.

Ryan saunters over to the freezer, pulls out the ice-cream tub and tears off the lid.

'We've literally just finished a double scoop from the mall,' says Brianne. 'Are you some kind of animal?'

'An animal annoyed that there's no chocolate left. Why don't we just buy chocolate? Why is it always Neapolitan?'

'Napoleon,' I say without thinking.

'It's Neapolitan, Lion. How many times?' Ryan protests. 'Napoleon was the French dude who got stuffed at Waterloo.'

'Napoleon was actually of Italian descent,' Brianne says.

'Whatever,' says Ryan and turns to me. 'Unbelievable – don't say a word for an entire day and when you do it's the wrong one.' He's half-smiling at me but it still hurts.

'I think it's cute,' says Brianne.

'Ariana Grande is cute. Calling ice cream after a war general is not cute!' He grabs a spoon and starts eating.

'Ariana Grande?' Brianne scoffs. 'No chance. You need to lower your expectations.'

Ryan ignores her and eats another mouthful.

I can't take any more of them, or their fighting, and turn to head upstairs. Between them they have made it all a whole lot worse.

'Don't go, Lion,' says Brianne. 'We can sort this out together.'

I stop in the doorway but don't turn round.

'I told you her secret,' I say sadly over my shoulder. As I speak, I hear Patch click-clacking across the kitchen, slowly making his way over to me. He knows Richa is lost too.

'We won't tell a soul,' says Ryan. 'Swear it.'

'But you did,' I say. 'You told Richa. I'm worse.

Richa trusted me and I still told. I can't even talk and I still told you both my best friend's secret. I've ruined it all.'

'Oh, Lion,' says Brianne and I hear the slip-slap of her flip-flops but this time it's not comforting.

'I want to be on my own,' I say and the noise of her shoes stops sharply.

'Leave him,' says Ryan, spluttering through a mouthful of ice cream.

'Don't tell me what to do,' snaps Brianne, 'and stop eating out of the tub. It's totally gross.'

'Shut up, *Mum*.'

Patch and I leave them to argue, heading upstairs into the furnace of my bedroom. I flop face down onto my bed and fight back the tears. This is the worst thing that has ever happened to me. It's even worse than being frozen at Theo's party. It's worse because it's all my own fault.

One of my arms is hanging off the side of the bed. I feel a damp nose nuzzle into the palm of my hand. It's amazing that Patch's nose can still be cold and wet despite all this heat, but it is. He licks gently at each one of my fingers in turn.

'What am I going to do, Patch?' I ask into my

pillow. The licking gets a little bit more frantic. I turn my head to look at him. Patch is joyful at this small gesture, lunging at my face to lick it. He has stinky, dog-food breath so I push him gently away, but the sight of him makes me feel a tiny bit better. Patch will always love me, no matter what I do. He loves me even if I can't perform or talk to strangers. He loves me even when I give away big, heavy, important secrets.

'There must be some way of showing her how sorry I am,' I say and Patch pricks his ears forward at me, tilting his head to one side.

I lie in my white nylon flares, in the unbearable heat, trying to think of a way to make it better. There must be something I can do to repair the damage. I can't bear the thought of going back to life before having Richa as my friend.

The noise of music floats up the stairs. At first I think Mum must be home, then I realise it's a bad Ryan joke. He's put on one of Mum's records: 'No Woman No Cry' by Bob Marley and the Wailers. I can hear my brother's terrible singing drowning out the lyrics.

The music stops abruptly.

'What are you doing? I was listening to that,' Ryan shouts.

'It's not funny,' Brianne shouts back.

But the music has given me an idea. I sit up and Patch gets up too, wagging his tail and panting at me. I know what I have to do. The only way to sort this mess out is to make myself perform tonight. I have to beat the SM, not for me, but for Richa.

The whole idea is terrifying. I could freeze. Richa might not even dance with me. I could be out there on my own, frozen.

The theatre will be packed. Everybody staring at the frozen freak on stage.

Panic builds as the image of me alone on stage, frozen, forms vividly in my mind. Remembering the advice of my speech therapist I take a few steadying breaths. I have to at least try. That was what upset Richa the most – that I didn't try. Even if I try and fail, at least I will show Richa how sorry I am and how much I want to be her friend. It is the idea of failing that is the most scary, but I can't think about that, I have to force it down.

I check the clock. One hour before we have to

be at the Library Theatre for tonight's performance. How can I even tell Richa what I've
got planned when I can't talk to her? What if she
doesn't turn up?

I suppose I could ask Brianne or Ryan for help.
If I tell them my plan, they could tell Richa. Then
I remember the look on her face. The hurt, the
betrayal. No, this has to come from me. Only me.

My eyes look past Patchy to my shelf of picture
books. *Bronco* is jutting out. I get up and pull the
book off the shelf. Maybe, just maybe Richa has
learnt enough words. If I only use the words
from *Bronco* then I can try and write her a note
to explain.

18

Dragging my school bag out from under the bed I find my pencil case inside. It has the smell of school attached to it: pencil shavings and feet. Opening it, I take out a highlighter pen.

I flick through *Bronco*, looking for the words that I need to say. My plan is that I will highlight them in turn then show them in the right order to Richa. Having a plan is good, it settles my nerves and makes me focus.

I try, but it's no good. There's no 'sorry' in the book, nor can I find 'dancing' or 'perform' or 'tonight'. I keep glancing at the clock. It's taking too long. If only I could just speak, then I could tell her.

This is a stupid idea. Frustrated I throw the book on the floor and sit back down on my bed. I feel useless and pathetic. Why can't I just talk? Why can't I be normal?

'Hello?' It's Mum.

Patch leaps up, galloping down the stairs to greet her.

'Anyone home? Apart from Patchy? Don't we have to leave soon?'

I hear a low rumble of voices and even though I can't work out what is being said it's obvious that they're talking about me. I don't move and the bad thoughts inside my head slosh around like dirty washing.

I hear Mum coming up the stairs, a gentle knocking on my open door.

'Hey Lion.' Mum's face peeps round the door.

'Hello,' I say.

Mum takes that as an invitation and comes into my and Ryan's bedroom. She smells of chip fat and, even though it's way too hot, she sits down next to me and puts an arm round my shoulders.

'Brianne told me you and Richa had a falling out,' Mum says into my hair.

'Yeah. It was my fault,' I say, hoping Brianne didn't tell Mum Richa's secret.

Mum cuddles me for a bit then says, 'Want me to be interpreter?'

Do I want this? Can I even do it? The letter would've been better, but that's not going to work, this might be the only chance I've got.

'OK,' I say, wondering what I can whisper into Mum's ear to make it better and not give Richa's secret away. The bad thoughts settle into a low rumble at the back of my mind now that there is another plan.

But when we get over to Richa's house nobody answers the door. I'm hopping from one foot to another wanting to see Richa and not wanting to see her at the same time.

'Maybe they've left already,' says Mum looking

at her watch. She sniffs at her uniform. 'I've got to have a quick five-minute shower before we go.'

I tap her on her shoulder and she offers her ear. 'What about Richa?' I whisper. We can't just leave things unsaid.

'It will blow over. She's a lovely girl.'

Mum walks back down the path. How can she say that? None of this will just blow over. I've got no choice but to follow Mum, but I know that Richa will never forgive me. I'm the worst friend in the world. The only way I can think of to try to make it right is completely terrifying, yet I'm determined to do it. I have to force myself to try. Performing is the only way to show Richa how sorry I am for breaking her trust. I hope she shows up. If she doesn't come tonight then I won't have to perform, but I'll know that I'll have lost her friendship forever.

While Mum has a shower, I do a few bounces on the trampoline. Patch comes with me – sadly sniffing under the fence for a future DogGirl who isn't there.

Bouncing up high I look over the third fence panel and see the empty trampoline. It's like I've made her disappear. The thought of what I've done stops my bouncing and I sit on the side of the trampoline, letting my white-flared trousered legs hang off the edge.

Nothing is fun without Richa.

What if what I've done makes her go away for real? What if she never starts at Lakeside and the family move away from Luton? I've got so used to all the sounds from their house, the delicious cooking smells from their kitchen. I've got used to Richa as my friend.

'You look super-funky in that outfit.' Ryan is standing in the doorway. He takes a picture of me with his phone and starts his slow, cowboy-style walk towards me. I'm not sure I want to see him or Brianne right now. I'm still angry with them both so I don't say anything back.

'I've been thinking,' he says getting closer. 'I feel bad about telling Richa what you told us. Maybe if me and Brianne had kept our mouths shut it wouldn't be so bad. To make it up to you,' he waggles his phone at me. 'I'm going to let you keep this bad boy.' He hands it to me. When our fingers touch there's a shock of static electricity.

It hurts.

'Woah,' Ryan says reeling backwards. 'That some fierce polyester you got going on there.'

I don't care that it hurt, I've got my own phone! I turn it over in my hands. It's hot to the touch. This makes up for everything both Ryan and Brianne said to Richa. I can't believe that I've got my own phone!

'It's a bit of an old timer and temperamental at times, but it does the job. I've been deleting any incriminating evidence. There's a couple of things I don't remember, like my wallpaper.' He looks up to smile knowingly at me. 'And this...' He gets close again, bending his head over the phone and I catch the sweet smell of his spray, fainter now.

I watch the screen as he opens the voice memos.

'Bronco,' he says, 'You'd think I'd remember a client with a name like that, but I've got nothing.'

Ryan motions as if to press play, but lifts his head up, makes his fingers into a gun and pretend shoots me instead. 'On the money that one, Lion,' he says and winks.

Risking another shock of static, I hug his head and shoulders because that's the only bit of my brilliant brother that I can reach sat up on the trampoline edge.

'Thank you, Ryan,' I whisper as I hug.

'Least I can do, little dude,' he says, his voice muffled from my hug. 'Richa's right. I'm well overdue an upgrade.'

I jump down with my new phone in my hand and run into our house, Patch at my heels. I'll need my dog for this new and improved plan. Patch can pretend to be Richa. Determination beats back my fear.

19

My family and I don't walk together with our new neighbours to the Library Theatre. There's still no sign of them.

'Maybe, they went out for tea first?' suggests Brianne, but I know she's really thinking the same as me. After what happened earlier, maybe Richa won't come at all. Would there be any point humiliating myself on my own if Richa isn't even there to see it? She has to come, she has to.

Mum, Ryan, Brianne and I, walk out of the

glare of the heatwave and into the library. Instantly, I'm thinking of the afternoon Richa and I spent getting books for her. I picture her face when she spotted words that she knew and I nodded to say she's got them right. She was so happy. I feel terrible for sharing her secret. Is it a worse feeling than the fear of having to dance in front of everyone? Different kind of bad. Just as bad.

I've been inside the library lots of times, but never into the theatre. I'm expecting something similar to the dance studios, kind of scruffy and makeshift, but this is something else. It's a proper theatre. The four of us walk into the auditorium which is beginning to fill. There's a smell of new fabric and anticipation. Quickly, I scan the blue-upholstered, fold-down seats, but there's no sign of Richa or her family.

'There's some space still on the front row,' says Mum. 'We'll get the best view, won't we, Lion?' She pulls me in for a sideways cuddle. Together we walk down the middle of all the seats towards the spotlight that shines on a purple curtain. I don't look at anyone, just keep my gaze on the light ahead. None of my family have any idea that I'm going to try to get up on that stage. Nobody does. The terror and determination battle it out inside my head like two sword fighters.

As we walk closer, the curtain moves, and noises of things happening filter out. I catch Call-Me-Felicity's voice and the tap of Anton's shoes.

'You better go backstage,' says Mum and her voice is all high and excited like a little kid at Christmas. 'You might be needed for props and things. I'll save your seat.'

My stomach flips over. Not my SM, not now. Go away, bully. I take a breath, in for five, out for five.

'I'll take you,' says Ryan, even though neither of us really know where to go. We climb up onto the stage and I follow my brother into the wings at the right. Once we're out of sight from the auditorium it's all very different. The air is thicker and tastes dusty, not at all like the fresh, air-conditioned clean smell of the auditorium. Black scaffolding poles crisscross one another with big boxy lights attached and wires are looped in and around everything.

We find the rest of the dance class and Felicity scattered in among it all. Everyone is dressed in their costumes and some are stretching or trying out different steps. There's no sign of Richa. I concentrate on my breathing.

'Hello Leo, my funky diva,' says Felicity. 'You can watch from backstage if you like.'

This is the moment when I have to come clean. As I tap on my brother's shoulder and he bends for me to whisper, I feel my throat tighten.

'I'm going to try to dance,' I croak.

He pulls back from me. 'You sure, Bruv?' he asks but I see the grin waiting to spread out across his face, just like the dancers in the wings waiting to go and perform.

I swallow down a huge lump of nerves and doubt. Blotting out the SM voice, I nod at my big brother.

Ryan turns to Felicity and says, 'He wants to dance. At least he wants to try to dance.'

Felicity's face lights up with an enormous smile. 'That's wonderful news. I'm so proud of you, Leo. You are the most beautiful dancer and now that you have Richa – well I can't wait to hear that applause. You two are destiny's dynamite.'

I give her a flicker of a smile, but I can't look right at her. It's too much. If Richa comes then I can't turn back now even if I do freeze. The sword fight inside my head intensifies.

'Want me to record it for you on your new phone?'

I look down at the phone in my hands, the hopeful headphones hanging from it. My brother offers his ear again. 'I need Richa to listen to something first,' I whisper.

He winks at me. 'I'll come back for it.'

I go to hug him again, but he backs off. 'Not risking that static shock, little dude,' he says. 'Bust a leg!'

As time passes and the auditorium fills, I anxiously watch backstage for Richa and her family. Unlike school, the seats fill from the front backwards and I see Tiffany with her mum, dad and sister sitting a few rows back from my family. No space has been left for me after all.

The noise of chatter gets louder, drowning out the hushed whispers that come from backstage.

It feels very real, and I try not to think about all those hundreds of staring eyes.

Then I spot Richa's mum, swaying from side to side with the weight of the baby, and pulling Aahan by his hand beside her. Next comes Richa's dad, talking on his phone walking in slow, wide circles by the auditorium doors. I look for Richa, thinking she might be with her dad but she's not.

'Hello Leo.'

I jump and turn. Richa is there right behind me. She's still in her sequinned outfit but she looks even more miserable than when she fled from our kitchen. Her eyes are all puffy, the gold eyeshadow completely gone and her wig isn't on straight. Everything rushes and tumbles inside me and I want to hold her and tell her how sorry I am – but I can't.

'Richa,' says Felicity, light-stepping to join us. 'I was beginning to worry that you weren't coming.'

'I thought about it,' admits Richa. 'Is it OK to watch from here?'

'Watch?' says Felicity. 'You can watch until it's your time to go on.'

'But…?' Richa glances at me, confused. 'I can't do the dance on my own. I tried that at the rehearsal and I looked stupid.'

'Ah, and that's why our wonderful Leo here will be dancing with you.' I'm looking at Richa waiting for her reaction but I can hear the smile in Felicity's words.

Richa's face changes from misery, to confusion, to disbelief.

'But you can't do it,' she says to me.

I shrug and make myself hold her eye.

'He can,' says Felicity and begins fixing Richa's wig properly. She has enough confidence for all of us. 'And he will. The first time is always the hardest, but I guarantee you will both shine like the most marvellous magic.'

Richa starts to smile, just softly. A pull at the corner of her mouth. 'Really?' she asks me. 'You're going to try to perform? For me?'

I nod and as Felicity disappears, with a shaking hand I lift the phone and headphones so she can see them.

'Ryan's phone?'

I shake my head and tap the phone into my chest.

'Your phone? Did he upgrade?'

I nod again.

She smiles properly now, as she tucks the left ear bud into her ear. 'He knows good advice when he hears it,' she says, and I smile back. This is more like the real Richa and I'm glad that determination is winning inside my head – at least for the moment.

Not needing or wanting to hear my voice, I let Richa have both earbuds so she can listen in stereo. It was only moments ago that I pretended Patch was Richa when I told him what I really wanted to tell her. I press play on the recording I made and labelled 'Sorry'.

Richa,

I'm really sorry for telling Ryan and Brianne your secret. I told them because they didn't understand. They didn't know that you couldn't read my letter.

They swore not to tell anyone. I know they won't because they didn't even tell Mum.

You're getting really good at reading now. If you

let me, I want to keep helping you and I'll never tell anyone else. I swear.

I can help you when you start at Lakeside.

Maybe we can help each other?

I'm going to dance tonight. I'm going to make myself do it because I know it will show you how sorry I am.

My SM is horrible and dancing in front of people will be really hard for me.

I'm so scared but I know I have to do it.

I want to do it, but the SM is like an enormous wall I have to climb over first.

It's hard to explain.

There's so much that I want to say to you, but I can't. Maybe now that I have this phone it might be a way that I can?

I can try. If you want?

There's one thing I really want to say.

Even though you couldn't read my letter sometimes it feels like you have. It's like you do understand. You are the best friend I have ever had, Richa.

That's why I'm going to dance.

I'm performing so that we can still be friends.

Richa takes the earphones out and her eyes are full of tears. She hugs me and I hug her back.

I hear her whisper in my ear, 'I'm sorry too.'

'Aw, you two are the cutest.' It's Brianne's voice. As we pull out of our hug I catch the scent of Brianne's shampoo. It smells familiar and good, like fresh hope. I can do this. I can.

Felicity dances over, 'You can't be back here now,' she stage-whispers to Brianne. 'We're about to start.'

'Sorry,' Brianne whispers back. 'Just came to collect the phone.' She takes the phone, winding the cable around it in a neat, quick movement. 'Got to make sure we record it all. Mum is beside herself with excitement.'

Brianne goes to move away and then she lifts the phone and takes a quick, sneaky photo of Richa and me. We're holding hands and I hadn't even noticed.

'Just the cutest,' she says.

'Go, go, go.' Felicity waves my sister away.

'Next stop *The Lion King*,' Brianne says as she disappears.

Richa laughs and gives my hand a little squeeze.

It's our time to dance.

I hide within my costume. I am not a boy who can't talk, I'm a new boy, one who was born to perform. This is what I tell myself to quieten the noise inside my head. This is what I have to believe in order to get out there in front of everyone.

There are no final words from Richa. She doesn't grab at me and try to pull me, like before. Instead, holding hands, we steadily walk out together from the wings into the middle of the dark stage. The audience is quiet, the music has not yet started and, closing my eyes for a moment, I tell myself to breathe. I remind myself not to listen to anything but the music, especially not any bad thoughts that might come.

I do not have to talk; I just have to dance.

I am not alone. I am with my best friend Richa and I am trying.

Here I am, trying my very best.

We're in our starting positions – backs to the audience, side-by-side, freeze-framed in the John Travolta pose. The spotlight blazes suddenly onto us, cooking our backs. It's as hot as the heatwave and our shadows cast out in front of us, up onto the curtain, like the perfect silhouette. I imagine from the audience we must look like one of Mum's album covers. Two members of Earth, Wind and Fire.

Because I can't see all the faces of the audience it's easier to block their staring eyes out of my mind.

I'm surprisingly calm, the SM bully quiet.

The music starts and immediately my automatic dance-pilot kicks in. Everything else disappears: the worry, the terror, the doubt. All thoughts of anything other than dancing slide away from me, like water running off my skin in the shower.

This is what this boy does – he dances.

Our routine is so well rehearsed we could do it in our sleep – and have. I let the music carry my body, moving it in practised perfection.

De dah de dah de dah de dah de da de da doh.
Doom da de doom da.

This boy is the Disco King!

Four Travoltas on each side, pivot turn and into the glare of the lights.

Egg beat roll, shoulder wiggle, rolling grapevine, funky chicken and groovy side-step left, then right, all the way through the introduction.

Doom da de doom da.

Doom da de doom da.

Shuffle, kick change, easy walk for three with arms, twist and lunge for the beat of four. Strut walk away from Richa, with New York mambo change and sassy finger click. Head jerk to strut walk back, high fiving Richa on the way past. Same back to the middle and into the chorus; the beat of the lyrics energising me.

Doom da de doom da. Deedo da dee-doh.

Synchronised Travoltas, with back-leg flick.

I'm grinning. I can feel it, wide across my face. Richa is too and we can hear them – the audience is singing. The beat is amplified by them.

Doom da de doom da. Deedo da dee-doh.

With more energy, we jump into part two, back-to-back, partner arm links and the back rolls, each letting the other roll over our backs as we rotate around in a full circle. There's cheering and clapping, I can hear it above the music.

We're the Disco King and Queen!

Into the strut walk and high fives, shuffle kicks with head and arm roll twists. Underwater wiggle with fingers holding noses, then grapevine with dandruff dust, and back into the chorus.

Doom da de doom da. Deedo da dee-doh.

They're singing, they're definitely singing. Did they do that for the others? Wait – they're up on their feet and dancing. The audience is dancing!

Doom da de doom da. Deedo da dee-doh.

Doom da de doom da. Deedo da dee-doh.

It's incredible but over too quick and now we're strutting and spinning our way off stage as the music fades. We can hear the cheering and stamping of feet.

'They loved us, Leo. They loved us!'

Richa is breathing heavily, her chest heaving up and down and she's grinning. Really grinning. All I know when we hug is that I have never felt so happy in my whole life. With her ear close to mine I whisper, 'We did it!'

She doesn't pull out of our hug. She doesn't jump up and down screaming that I finally spoke to her. It's like she knew that I would always talk to her, if she just waited long enough because, she just whispers back in my ear softly, 'We did.'

20

It's three days after the performance and there's
no more Just Jive. We won the voucher and Richa
got her dance shoes. The glory of our triumphant
dance on stage surrounded us for a while, but
now that Richa's mum has gone into hospital to
have her baby, all the attention has shifted away.

Performing with Richa was a huge thing for
me to do. Mum and Brianne were both in floods
of tears, and even Ryan looked a bit choked up.
They pretty much told anyone and everyone

about it, whether they were interested or not. I even heard Mum telling the milkman this morning.

It was completely special and, now that I have it as a memory, I know I will be able to use it. Instead of thinking about Theo's birthday party, I can remember how the audience got up to dance and sing along to 'Disco Inferno'. I can remember the 'on top of the world' feeling of being up on that stage with Richa dancing in perfect harmony. Even if I never make it any further with my dancing, I will always have the 'Disco Inferno' dance.

It wasn't *The Lion King*, but I did it – the evidence is on my phone. It was also especially satisfying to see the shocked look on Scarlett and Maryam's faces. Richa said that was the best bit, like our dance had slapped them both good and proper.

Richa and I are underneath my trampoline, with books, ice pops and a snoozing Patchy. It smells of scorched earth, sticky sugar and sun-baked dog. Richa is copying the words she has learned into a notepad she took from her dad's work supplies. The cover of the notebook has the name of one of the pharmaceutical drugs he sells, *Herceptin*, stamped on it, and its little yellow logo on each page.

We're waiting to hear baby news from the hospital. Mum is next door, babysitting Aahan. He can't come to our house because of Patch. They're icing the 'congratulations' cake they made together. We can hear the radio, faint and distant, coming from Richa's kitchen.

Richa has made the notebook into a home-made dictionary, three pages for each letter of the alphabet, but she's not written the meaning of the words, just the words themselves. We've got three weeks left of the summer holidays and she's determined to learn as much as she can before starting at Lakeside. Brianne and Ryan both think it's better if Richa is honest with the head teacher, Mrs Malik, but nobody pushes her. Neither of Richa's parents know; it's still a secret between the four of us.

Richa has been talking about Lakeside more now that Just Jive has finished. Starting there worries her, I can tell by how quiet she goes when she's thinking about it.

'What's Mrs Malik like?' Richa asks me.

I put a thumb up.

'Just one thumb?'

I nod, she's a head teacher after all.

Neither of us say anything for a while, as Richa flicks through the copy of *The Gruffalo's Child* that she's learnt off by heart. I watch as she writes *scared* into her dictionary.

'Did you tell her about your SM?' Richa asks at last.

I ear whisper that Mum did.

Richa mulls that over a while in her mind, flicking through the pages filled with snowy pictures and chewing on the end of her pencil. She copies out the word *brave*. I suck the rest of my ice-pop reading over her shoulder.

'If it was your choice, would you have told her?' Richa asks me.

I think about that before I answer. There's no way of hiding my SM, not at school anyway, and trying to keep it a secret would probably make it worse for me. If I didn't want people to know it would add to my stress and worry. Once people understand that I can't talk to them they no longer expect me to talk. That does mean that I often disappear into the background. Sometimes it's almost like I'm not there at all, but that's better than feeling the pressure of expectant eyes when someone asks me a question that I can't answer.

I tap Richa on the shoulder and she leans over so I can ear whisper.

'Mrs Malik organised help for me and my SM,' I say, thinking about my speech therapist and the whiteboard I can use to write on instead of speaking.

Richa nods at this. She's quiet as she thinks. Patchy snores softly and the radio noise drifts through the heatwave. I feel totally at peace and if I lay down and closed my eyes, I could easily fall asleep.

'I'm going to tell her,' Richa says finally and, as if to confirm her decision, she drinks the rest of her melted ice-pop from the wrapper. Tipping it right up, she lets the sweet liquid pour in and the bright blue stains her mouth.

This is the right decision for Richa to make and I'm glad. Once Mrs Malik knows how we are helping one another I know she'll support us. Maybe she'll become a two thumbs-up head teacher after all. Having Richa with me in Year Six is going to make school so much better. I just hope the heatwave is over by then.

'It's a girl!' Mum shouts over the fence, making us jump and waking Patchy up.

'Yes!' shouts Richa, punching our trampoline ceiling. Patchy sneezes as his own doggy celebration.

'Both doing great – be home in a couple of hours. We know what to write on the cake now!'

'A sister,' Richa says to me and grins.

I smile back, but there's a tiny niggle of worry that Richa will be more interested in her new sister than me. Babies can't go to school, I remind myself. Babies can't do much of anything at all. Richa goes back to *The Gruffalo's Child*.

'Sister isn't in this book. Can you show me how to write it?'

I watch her turn to the S pages in her dictionary. Lots of different words are written, but not in the right order: *special, shade, shouted, shiny, show-ring, saved, snow, short*. Taking

Richa's pencil, next to her last word on the list, *scared*, I write: *sister*.

Richa sounds out the letters: S-I-S-T-E-R.

'You're the best friend ever,' Richa says and smiles at me. 'I'll be OK at Lakeside because you'll be with me. Thanks, Leo.'

I know for definite that there's nothing temporary about Richa, nothing at all. I lean in again and she offers me her ear. It curves in a perfect shape, like a wishing seashell you might find on the beach if you're lucky. My lips are close enough to brush her skin and as I say the precious words, it's like I'm making a wish, or maybe keeping a promise.

'Call me Lion.'

About Selective Mutism (SM)

Leo has a condition called Selective Mutism or SM, but what does that mean exactly and how can you help?

SM is a disability but not one that is immediately obvious. It's a kind of phobia, but instead of being frightened of heights or tight spaces, children with SM are scared to talk.

Children with SM are physically capable of talking and they want to but in certain situations they can find it impossible. They may use other ways to communicate such as nodding or shaking their heads, pointing, or writing things down. Most children with SM are able to talk when they are in familiar, safe places and with the people who know them best. Other environments, such as school, are often too difficult and frightening for children with SM to be able to talk.

If you know someone with SM, or there is a quiet child in your school there are a few things to remember and ways that you can help to make them feel more confident.

- Don't try to get them to speak or ask them direct questions. This can make them feel extremely anxious and will make the situation worse.
- Remember that pairs or small groups, especially with close friends is a much more comfortable way of working and playing.
- Include them, don't ignore them. Children with SM want to join in, so make sure you don't leave them until last if you're picking teams. Invite them to sit with you and include them in what you're doing.
- Don't mimic or laugh at them. This is extremely hurtful and unkind.
- If and when they do speak, do what Richa did and don't make it into a big deal. The more relaxed and safe they feel with you, the more likely it is that they will talk.
- Be patient.
- Be kind.

This information was taken from the SMiRA leaflet for primary schools: What Is SM? If you're affected by SM or want to know more about the condition please visit: www.selectivemutism.org.uk

Acknowledgements

This is the part where I get to thank everyone who has been involved in bringing *Call Me Lion* to life. I always read this section when I finish a book and it's usually filled with mentions of agents, editors, illustrators, designers, writing colleagues, friends and family. Whilst I am hugely grateful to all of these people (you know who you are) I want to dedicate this space to the children, families and professionals who helped me that are directly affected by Selective Mutism.

In order to do that I need to tell you the story behind *Call Me Lion*. Usually it's a story idea that comes to me but in this case it was Lion himself who arrived in my head as a fully formed boy. He talked to me incessantly, but when I sat down to write his story I realised he was *only* talking to me. I began researching into why he wasn't talking and discovered the rare condition of Selective Mutism (SM). I drafted the book but, knowing I needed help, I reached out to an organisation that supports families affected by SM called SMiRA (Selective Mutism Information & Research Association).

I received amazing advice which was instrumental in shaping *Call Me Lion*. I'm eternally grateful to everyone who stuck with me. The book is finally here! Those who need special acknowledgment are: Sam Smith (and her mum Dawn), Molly Patel, Catherine and Daniel Bates, Charlie Rose Hill, Lindsay Whittington, Laura Whittell and Mia Whittell.

Through SMiRA I also met Donna Redrup and learned the heart-wrenching story of her son James. James struggled with SM throughout his childhood and sadly died of Sudden Onset Leukaemia just before his 25th birthday. This book is dedicated to his memory.

Lion has always been a very real and loveable boy, not just to me but to everyone who has met, or is about to meet him. This is his story, he's just found me tell it for him and I feel very honoured to have been chosen.

Thank you Lion!

Fun Facts about Camilla Chester:

1. She walks loads of dogs as a real job.
2. She likes dancing (even though she's not that great at it).
3. She's done well in some writing competitions.
4. She loved writing this book and got lots of help from kids with selective mutism.
5. She's really chatty and talks almost as much as Richa.
6. She lives close to Luton.
7. She grew up in Norwich with her mum, two older brothers and an older sister.
8. She laughs a lot and is a big pancake fan!

To find out more about Camilla you can visit her website: www.camillachester.com

Get your free printable bookmark!

Head to fireflypress.co.uk/blog/patch-bookmark or scan the QR code to get your free printable bookmark!

Happy folding!